THROWING SHADOWS

A DARK COLLECTION

Throwing Shadows sends you into a darkness in which Roth doesn't just plunge a dagger into your heart, but delights in adding a deliciously vicious twist. His nine chilling tales encompass a range of human failings, inviting evil through the door as a consequence. Sacrifice and betrayal, demonic possession and a dash of redemption ensure a mix to satisfy any horror reader. The ending to "The Keepsake" in particular, is one I will not forget in a hurry. Dare you step into the shadows?
—Stephanie Ellis, author of *The Five Turns of the Wheel*

THROWING SHADOWS

A DARK COLLECTION

Jerry Roth

Brigids Gate
PRESS

For my wife Tricia, who taught me that life is a journey and not a destination.

This book is in memory of Molly Carter. Her love of movies and books showed me the value of art. She was a bright light in a dark world. Ninety-nine years wasn't enough

ALSO BY JERRY ROTH

Bottom Feeders

On the Tip of Her Tongue

CONTENTS

A Woman's Strength 1

Always Say Goodbye 19

The Keepsake 37

Whispers from the Cellar 53

The Idiot Box 71

The Teddy Bear 87

Ice Cream Man 101

My Soul to Take 109

Lightning Crashes 121

About the Author 137

About the Illustrator 139

Acknowledgements 141

More From Brigids Gate Press 143

~ A WOMAN'S STRENGTH ~

Lush cornfield filled Sara's bedroom window and made the world green. The scarecrow in the center of her view every dawn made Sara uneasy. But what frightened her most was the darkness when she couldn't see it.

Pressing Shelly close to her breast, she had a fleeting hope that this was going to be the time everything clicked. The child hadn't taken to breastfeeding, and things had gotten worse with each attempt. Shelly scrunched up her face and squirmed away as usual. She lay her fussy eater down, hopes dashed once more.

Closing her shirt, Sara thought how marriage had taken her from the city life and, worse than that, proved how fragile she was. Women were strong enough to run plantations all on their own. But did Sara have that depth? Not being able to feed her child brought doubt to her doorstep.

She felt small on the new journey. *I need instructions.* Sara readied herself for a day of disappointments.

The baby's cradle had always been next to her and her husband's bed. *Fresh air is important for a child*, her mother-in-law suggested. She tried to think of a reason to keep the child close but the excuses alluded her, so she placed the cradle next to the window so the breeze would caress baby Shelly.

She loved Nancy like a mother, even if she wasn't. Sara's parents died five years before she met Jacob. When her daughter was born, Nancy swooped in when she was at her lowest and helped them make sense of being a parent. Without any thought for herself, Nancy offered to stay with them as they adjusted to a new baby. She had years of experience raising children and Sara clung to every morsel.

Sara lifted Shelly from her cradle and spotted movement from the corner of her eye.

The scarecrow's head faced her and the baby. *The stuffed head aimed the other way before.* She was positive. *Lack of sleep?* Shelly's fussiness continued as Sara drew the shade closed and headed out of their bedroom.

In the kitchen, Sara listened to Jacob whistling as he always did. Not a care in the world. Nancy piled food onto plates the way Sara used to every morning. The responsibility of breakfast had left her like a wisp. One day she made all the family meals and the next... food sat waiting for her.

The shift in home duties lifted the burden, but another idea pestered. *What will I do?* It hurt seeing her mother-in-law fill her shoes so easily. Across the table, Sara watched Jacob stuff scraps into his mouth, unaware of her turmoil boiling inside.

"He won't latch on." Annoyance was back on Sara's face with the second attempt at feeding. "She's acting like my milk's bad." Sara hit the kitchen table with her palm and worried about the fate of her child.

Nancy was a Kansas tornado. Blowing in to wrap Shelly within her arms.

"We have plenty of baby formula in reserve," Nancy said. "Shelly's got to eat. And so do you." She hoisted a plate with one hand and balanced Shelly in the other. Sliding the plate forward, Nancy centered a breakfast in front of Sara. "I gotta earn my keep here. I'll feed the baby. You enjoy the morning." The older woman spread her lips and revealed yellowed teeth.

Sara started a smile at the woman's gentle words, but it died before ever appearing. "I guess I haven't been eating much lately," Sara said and stared at her distracted husband. A newspaper border divided them. She opened her mouth to speak and closed it as fast.

"I think I'll finish my food outside. In the sunshine," he announced and scooped up his plate full of proteins, kissed Sara on her cheek, and shuffled through the screen door. Sara eyed her mother-in-law mixing baby formula a second before she followed Jacob.

She made it as far as the doorway before the spring closed her inside. Jacob was halfway toward his field of corn when she pressed her nose to the screen. He walked to the edge of the crops with his plate, then sat, crossing his legs as his butt met the ground.

Sara drifted her eyes upward and saw the scarecrow just above Jacob, a few feet into the field, on his pole. As the scarecrow and her husband faced each other, she felt a chill.

His family held a value in the stuffed creature she would never understand. When Jacob's anxiety was at its worst, she heard him speaking to the stuffed man, bouncing off ideas, and she swore he prayed to the thing.

Ridiculous. But there he was, talking about his morning with a scarecrow instead of his wife.

It was closer to morning by the time Jacob crawled into bed. The outer fringes of sleep faded until she sensed he was beside her, fast asleep.

She gave a nudge with no prayer of him waking. He worked until dusk countless times—but late into the night? That hadn't happened very often. Although she was new to farming, it was peculiar that anything kept him busy so late. *Something must have gone wrong.*

The few seconds that stirred her sleep were all it took to awaken the rest of her senses. It was no accident when Shelly popped into her mind as she always did. The nights were worse, and her thoughts were alive with worry. Was she hungry? Was she breathing? Was she dressed warm enough? Those thoughts, along with a half-dozen others, kept her on edge when what she needed was rest.

Did Jacob check in on Shelly? She didn't think so. He often dove into bed—near exhaustion every night without a glance her way. Leaving the concern and burden to her.

Thousands of years of motherly intuition set a fire in her brain, giving her a paranoia that something was wrong with her child. Even as she checked in on her nightly and found her fine, she couldn't shake the fear. An ugly anxiety slipped over her.

The breeze from the window fluttered the shade over the cradle as she headed for Shelly. She already planned a glass of water and a trip to the bathroom afterward when she stopped in her tracks.

Moonlight through the window was enough to see the spot the baby slept was empty. Sara squinted as if the girl would come into focus from sheer willpower alone. The bed remained vacant, and panic was a stalking animal trapped in the room with her. Sara searched beside the cradle as if the child, who couldn't sit up by herself, had somehow climbed over the side.

Her heart sank when Shelly wasn't on the floor, but relief washed over her that she wasn't laying there, injured from the fall. Her mind worked fast, and that was her problem. Too many ideas came in, clogged her brain, and stalled her reason.

More desperate than ever, Sara searched the room until movement drew her attention. There was flailing, except it wasn't in the room. Through the open window, she saw Shelly lying on the grass a few feet from the knee-high stalks of corn.

Seeing her baby out in the elements melted the fog— determination replaced her dreamy motions long enough for her to pump her legs toward the front door. She shouted to Jacob sleeping in the bed and to Nancy down the hall.

Shifting to a higher speed, her foot slipped, but her socks found traction in time to keep from falling headfirst. The closed door stopped her momentum. With hands scrambling with the knob, she turned and pulled it free.

The night wind, cold and harsh, pressed against her face. Her initial thought was the breeze tried to keep her from Shelly. The idea was ridiculous, far-fetched, but it also grabbed onto some dark part of her psyche that told her Shelly wasn't long for the world. Seeing the helplessness of the girl minutes after birth showed her the frailty of life.

Sara found another gear as she rushed toward the corner of the house. The moon, high above the cornfield, shone down on the grass.

She saw the naked child nestled on the soft earth. How long had Shelly been there? Her skin shimmered from the light creeping through the stalks.

Something moved in the field. Whatever it was, took up a lot of space and darkened the form of her baby.

Her feet moved before she understood what cast the blackness. And as she moved closer, so did the shadow. When Shelly was within reach, the stars disappeared altogether. Sara clutched her girl in the chilly air, expecting an attack. *Is this it? I'm not ready to die.* The idea of death got her feet moving, even if hopelessness threatened to pull them both down.

Shelly lay on Sara's warm chest. The problem remained the same—whatever made its way toward Shelly wasn't giving up without a fight. With every movement of her legs, the sound of scratching rose from behind. When she slowed, the scratching mimicked her movements.

Sara stretched her neck upward and screamed into the night. A glow came from the house. The scratching sped up and for a split second, she thought it was upon them. Instead, the sound moved away. Or did it?

With the thud of rushing feet, Sara watched light throwing shadows toward the cornfield. Hands grabbed her from behind— powerful limbs. A scream was in her throat, then she realized the hands were Jacob's.

"You're going to be fine. I got you," Jacob said. The moon's light bathed his body and showed the contour of his muscles.

Farm work had chiseled his arms and shoulders like nothing else could.

Pressed against him, Sara walked through the yard and took one last glance toward the scarecrow. To her surprise, it no longer stood above the cornfield.

As tears filled her eyes, the blur of wavering corn disappeared, and Jacob led her back into the house.

Without ever knowing it could happen, Sara found herself on trial that morning. She turned and saw Jacob's face. There was something else below the surface that made his appearance so odd. It was him against her. No one spoke aloud, of course, but she felt his accusing expressions just the same.

"I know what I saw. It was standing over Shelly. It wanted her," Sara said.

"Keep your voice down."

"I don't care if your mother hears me. I'm inside my house now. Not hers."

"I know. No one's saying it's not yours." With every comforting word, Sara's anger flared. "All I'm saying is that you haven't slept as you should. And scarecrows don't…"

"Don't what? Move? Are you saying I'm crazy?" she screamed.

Jacob lowered his chin to the floor, then at Shelly asleep in the small space of her wicker bassinet.

"I'll show you." Sara moved to the window. She reached over Shelly, who cooed in her sleep. She pulled down the shade and watched it slide up in a flash; the rolling material sounded like birds as it fluttered toward the top of the window frame.

Through the window, she saw the scarecrow perched high above the stalks of corn.

Jacob opened his mouth to speak, but closed it just as fast.

"I know he moved," she said, and studied the outline of its form against the background of the crops.

"The scarecrow—made generations ago by someone in the family—has watched over us and this farm for hundreds of years. There's not a person in town who doesn't know our history. The scarecrow is as important to the land as the bare soil that feeds our corn." When Jacob finished, Sara broke her gaze from the cloth figure through the glass.

At first, she wondered if he was putting her on. He was a hardworking, serious man who wasn't prone to jokes. *So why speak about a stuffed man with such reverence?* She scooped up Shelly and held her close.

"I don't want Shelly sleeping next to the window. I don't want this window open at all," Sara said. She felt the defeat in her words. What *did* she want before she spat out the compromise? Seeing it thrown into the thresher or set ablaze in a bonfire?

"Absolutely." Jacob grabbed the bassinet and moved it away from the window.

His agreeable nature made her feel like a mental patient. And wasn't that what she was? Was it her who carried Shelly outside in her sleep and crawled back into bed? *What about the shadow thing? Did it really exist?* She felt like the cause of all their troubles.

"There. Problem solved. We keep the window closed and we keep Shelly much closer to our bed," Jacob said and tried on a fragile smile.

Sara didn't let Shelly out of her sight, carrying her the entire day. Nancy did her best to protest the act of defiance, but nothing her mother-in-law said penetrated the fear what she might suffer if she left the child alone.

Deep into the night, Sara slept while propped against the headboard, jerking herself back awake whenever she realized sleep had taken her. *You stay awake!* She gazed at the closed window. Knowing the scarecrow stood on the other side made her skin crawl. Shelly breathed in and out, her tiny chest pushing up and down. The distraction that wouldn't go away. Sara rechecked if she locked the windows and had no will to stop herself.

With the house quiet and no one awake, this was her moment to eat. She'd put it off all day and her rumbling stomach would wait no longer.

When she moved from the bedroom to the kitchen, she felt the invisible cord that connected her to Shelly, a tether heightened by recent events.

Sara moved through the kitchen with moonlight to help her along the way. She thought about the scarecrow facing their bedroom, with Shelly so near to it. She shook her head and felt the dreary cobwebs fall away.

Nancy had made a roast that night that Sara had refused earlier. Now her hunger took control. One arm swung the refrigerator door wide while another pulled the casserole dish full of cold roasted beef from its shelf.

She tore off a patch of beef before she even found the cushion of the kitchen chair. One handful after another, she plunged the meat into her mouth and that's when she felt whatever made the shadow—watching her. She pushed the thought away and ignored the goosebumps that rose on her arms.

With each tear of the beef, the blackened form awoke in her mind. *What were you?*

She scooped up chilled carrots and potatoes, which sat beside the roast, and shoved them in. The base sensation of eating drowned out everything and surely the reason she never felt the table move.

The window that gazed out into the yard stole her attention. There was a vibration in it that distorted the reflection. Glassware moved and shuddered behind the cabinets, matching the wobble of the kitchen table. Roast beef slid from her fingertips, forgotten as she saw everything around her turn into a carnival funhouse.

Pulling herself from a chair, Sara stood on uneasy legs. The lights turned on and then flickered. Shaking grew stronger as cabinets opened and swung as if by invisible hands.

A voice told her to fall to the ground—crawl for safety but she resisted.

Walking with unsteady footing, she moved to the kitchen sink just as the faucet let loose a stream of water into the basin. Its hiss rose even above the sound of glass jittering in a circle around her.

The flicker of light made a strobe effect and warped the movements of her arm as it reached for the kitchen faucet. The water coming out was hot—steaming the window—fogging her view to the outside. When her fingers reached the faucet, she sensed her hand touch another. The unexpected sensation caused her to withdraw as if discovering a slithering snake.

Her gaze dropped as the lights went out for good. The funhouse excitement ended. Cabinets found their former stillness, and the flow of water dried up. But the fog in the windowpane remained.

Her head drooped, confused by the quietness. Two red eyes watched her from the other side of the window. The eyes jolted her backward off her feet. Her hands wouldn't cushion her fall as her head hit the edge of the kitchen table.

Nancy came into view when Sara opened her eyes. She saw the woman talking without sound. A television stuck on mute. The older woman pulled Sara to a sitting position next to her enemy, the country dinette set. The sound came through at last.

"Can you hear me, dear?"

"I can hear you," Sara said without moving her body an inch. She had a floaty feeling, like she existed as a voice with a form tethering her. "What happened?" she asked and remembered the glowing red eyes.

"You tell me," Nancy said.

"The house started shaking. From floor to ceiling."

"I was resting just down the hall. I never felt a thing." Nancy angled her head the way a dog does when it's trying to understand.

Sara found her body was the same again and swiveled around the kitchen.

"Look at the cabinet doors. They're all open."

"Yes, they are." Nancy's condescending tone was too much.

"And there were eyes. Burning red eyes." The wrinkled hands of the old woman brought Sara to a standing position.

"I believe you," Nancy said, examining Sara's head like a nurse. "You got a nasty bump. I have aspirin in my medicine cabinet. Help yourself while I check on Shelly." Nancy had already vanished into another part of the house as her last word landed.

Sara could do nothing but laugh. A distant pounding in her head bloomed into a *skull thumper*, as her father used to say.

As she moved to the spare bathroom, now her mother-in-law's, she wondered why she listened to Nancy's directions at all. While Nancy checked in on *her* baby, she fetched medicine. Every time she gained some independence, her defiance melted away. By the time she reached the medicine cabinet and the aspirin within, Sara felt defeated.

With two tablets in her palm, she placed the bottle back on the shelf. That's when she spotted a barely visible bottle. It wasn't her medicine cabinet, but she couldn't resist the curiosity. She slid lotion to the side to expose a vitamin bottle with the word LIPASE.

The name of the supplement meant nothing to her. There were thousands of vitamin types out there in the grocery aisle. What struck her was that Nancy wasn't a believer in vitamins— quite the opposite. Nancy swore that eating the right foods would always do the trick. *So why have Lipase?*

A cry filled the air and cut through her thinking.

How could she stand there worrying about vitamins when Nancy was taking care of her child? The urgency for her baby's safety renewed, Sara ran for her child, each wail pulsing in her frame as a live wire.

She found Nancy walking around the living room with Shelly asleep in her arms.

"Why was she crying?"

"She wasn't crying."

"A moment before I walked in here, she was just screaming. I heard her," Sara said without understanding.

Nancy lifted a finger to her lips but kept a steady pat on the girl's back.

With the child's cries still ringing in her ears, Sara gazed around the room. "What's happening to me?"

"You're tired. And haven't eaten. I warned you. A mother must fill her tank first if she ever wants to nourish a child. Go to bed! I'll watch over Shelly."

Sara nodded and obeyed.

Sara slept, but it wasn't peaceful. The eyes returned in her dreams. Her intention to rest, then tackle the day evaporated.

Instead, she made it to the kitchen in a groggy daze. Jacob was reading the paper as usual, with his mom holding Shelly and piling food onto plates. Nancy had taken back the power and Sara was a passenger once again.

"I wanna feed my baby!" Sara announced. Jacob pulled his newspaper away from his face and Nancy froze in place.

"What's wrong with you?" Jacob asked.

"I just want my baby," Sara said, pretending she didn't understand her husband's question.

Nancy gave Jacob an uneasy expression as she passed Shelly to her mother.

"Are you hungry, sweetie?" She aligned the baby's head and spine.

When Shelly touched Sara's skin, she lifted her chin to root for milk.

"She's trying," Sara said with a smile. A moment later, the baby lost herself in her mother's milk. "She latched perfectly."

"See, I told you. Just be patient," Jacob said.

Sara nodded her agreement, but stopped when Shelly's suckling grew louder. A smacking sound started as she shook her head back left, then right.

"What's wrong with her?" The thrashing continued until Shelly turned her head away from the breast altogether. Milk spilled from her mouth as her cries rose.

Nancy was there to help, as always. She plucked the child so fast from Sara's arm that she didn't have time to refuse. Sara had the appearance of someone hit by a car.

"I don't understand," Sara said. She stared down at her bare breast, slid a finger over a drop of milk, and brought it to her tongue. A scowl twisted her expression. "It's sour." She went in for another taste. "Why does it taste so bad?" She directed her question to Jacob and got silence.

"It's what you're eating…or not eating," Nancy said with a smile as she rocked Shelly for comfort. "It always comes down to that."

Sara shifted to her husband and saw his eyes as they became saucers. If she expected him to say something to his mother, it didn't happen. He shrugged. Sara clenched her teeth and ran to her bedroom.

"Let her go," she heard Nancy warn Jacob. "She needs the rest."

Sleep was what Sara needed. It's what her body begged for since Shelly was born. But when she lay her head on her pillow, sleep felt so far away. She thought of her poor baby refusing a meal and her mind fell back to Nancy, blocking her at every pass until sleep took mercy on her.

She stood at the foot of a bed—her bed with two forms under the covers. She thought she was watching herself and Jacob when she realized the bed was different. The bedspread she picked from an online catalog was now an old-fashioned quilt.

Even the walls had aging wallpaper. She spun around what she thought was her room until…

The floor shook. The walls—or house itself—tilted like a teeter-totter. She imagined she was on an ocean liner way out to sea, swaying on the waves. A structure that was so strong appeared as flimsy as a sheet of paper. Pictures fell from the walls. Combs, brushes, and bottles of perfume slid off the vanity. The curtain rod gave way to reveal the scarecrow standing outside the window.

Sara screamed, but her shriek was nothing more than background noise in the quivering home. The two figures in bed propped themselves up against the headboard—clutching one another tight.

Sara couldn't believe her eyes. It was Nancy lying in front of her. Gone were her wrinkles. Her hair was the color of a golden sunrise. No more than twenty years of age, she guessed.

Next to her was Horace, Jacob's father. He had been dead long before she met Jacob, but she recognized him from pictures. The frightened couple didn't see Sara. They stared straight through her at the scarecrow in the window.

"What's happening, Horace?" Nancy demanded.

When Sara turned, the scarecrow was gone. But in a blink it was back. This time, standing next to the bed and a cradle—the same one Shelly called her own. Sara dared to step closer to the scarecrow and peeked inside. A tiny child lay sleeping within.

The scarecrow turned toward Sara and shook his head; bright red eyes glowed in the bedroom.

"You can see me? How can you see me?"

The scarecrow ignored the question and turned back toward the bassinet.

"What are you?" Nancy shouted.

"It's okay. We're going to be fine," Horace said.

Nancy's eyes went wide.

"What have you done?"

The scarecrow took a step forward with outstretched hands.

"Stay away. Don't you touch my baby!" When Nancy moved to block the scarecrow, Horace held her back.

"It's for the best," Horace promised.

When the scarecrow snatched the baby into its arms, Nancy let out a scream that made Sara cover her ears. The scarecrow nodded with Horace nodding back. A silent exchange between the two.

The scarecrow walked away with the tiny child and Nancy screamed louder than ever.

Sara woke to sweat-drenched clothes.

"Lipase," she said aloud and typed the word into her phone. What came back made her drop it into her lap. She searched the room to find she was alone. No Jacob and no Shelly. Tearing the blanket off, Sara ran for the door.

Making her way from the kitchen, something stopped her. She turned toward her knife set and slid the biggest one from the wooden block; a butcher knife. With the home empty, she had one place to check. Outside.

A breeze came from the harvest. The wind caressed her skin when she looked up to the moon. Sara gripped the knife and moved behind the house. She knew what awaited her. Turning the corner, she saw them—her family.

The entire scene was like a baptism. The scarecrow stood before them the way a priest might hold a ceremony. Jacob kneeled on one knee while Nancy held Shelly in her arms, ready to hand her over at a moment's notice.

"Stop!" All heads turned to Sara, and she tucked the knife behind her back—not ready to show her advantage. "I saw the lipase in your medicine cabinet," Sara said and edged closer. "It's an enzyme. You've been adding it to my food. Haven't you, Nancy?"

Jacob turned to his mother.

"Is that true?" Jacob asked as he stood. Nancy shook.

"Too much lipase and a mother's milk will change—making it sour. You've done everything to break the bond between me and Shelly."

The scarecrow remained fixed on the baby.

"I did it to help you."

"The way Horace *helped* you?"

The comment landed onto Nancy like a slap.

"You know nothing," Nancy said, but her voice undercut her confidence.

"He showed me last night." Sara pointed to the scarecrow. Its eyes glowed bright red. "Horace sacrificed Jacob and you let him." Sara stood a few feet away from the ceremony and made a move to slide closer.

"It wasn't Jacob. It was his sister," Nancy said.

Jacob lowered his head, but Sara was sure he'd heard the tale before.

"Why?"

"I didn't know this when I joined the family. Just like *you* didn't. But this is how it's done. Going back generations. Do you think it's an accident, the amount of crops this land gives us every year while the rest of the farms go under?"

"Crops? This is about a harvest?"

"Not one. A lifetime of harvests that have ensured our survival."

"The price is too high, Nancy."

"I wanted to soften the blow. Break your connection with the child. I tried to make it easier for you," Nancy said and held Shelly tighter.

"What are you getting for your soul?" Sara motioned to the scarecrow, and it stared back.

"A blood sacrifice is what's required. If we own the land, nothing bad will happen to us. I've seen it with my own eyes," Nancy said. The creature gave something of a smile from behind its canvas mask.

"You knew about this, Jacob, and never told me?"

"It's our way. It's always been our way."

"I'm not letting you take my baby," Sara said and revealed her knife to the moonlight.

Nancy took a step backward.

"We can have another, Sara. We'll get past this and have a son. I promise," Jacob said.

"Will Shelly feel anything?" Sara said and lowered her blade.

"Nothing. She won't feel a thing. You have my word." Jacob pulled Sara into his arms.

"It hasn't been the sacrifices that have kept this farm alive," Jacob whispered into her ear. "It's been the strength of the women." Jacob placed his lips on Sara's mouth and kissed her.

The scarecrow studied the exchange.

Sara was sure he had watched these events play out countless times through the ages. She tasted the sweetness of Jacob's kiss, then the acrid taste of copper. She saw his frightened eyes when she pulled away. The knife sunk deep under his jaw.

With a quick motion, the blade came out of Jacob cleanly. She plunged it into his thigh with a dexterity she never thought she possessed.

"No," Nancy screamed as Jacob dropped to his knees—still clutching his injured jaw.

"If a sacrifice is necessary, you'll be making one for Shelly and me."

Jacob lifted his head to her—blood dripped from between his fingers. "I think it's time this farm knows a woman's strength," she said and kicked Jacob toward the scarecrow. Jacob's eyes opened wide in terror. Nancy was in shock.

"You were wrong in the past. My daughter will be in control of her destiny."

When Sara turned from Nancy to the scarecrow, they nodded together. Something private passed between the two like an echo from an old book. As the scarecrow pulled Jacob into the cornfield, Sara took Shelly back into her arms. They listened to the gurgled screams of Jacob as he disappeared behind the row of corn stalks.

"Don't worry. You won't feel a thing."

~ ALWAYS SAY GOODBYE ~

Decades of dust lay in the home's attic. Although the house was beautiful in every detail—hand-carved moldings and marble adorned surfaces—the attic told a different story. Matt glimpsed forgotten furniture and heirlooms resting at its highest level—waiting for a chance to shine again.

"There are enough cobwebs to sew a quilt," his father Peter said.

"Don't joke about such things," his mother Victoria said as she studied the room for any creepy crawlers.

"You okay, Matt?" Peter called out in the dark.

"This is fun!" the thirteen-year-old answered with too much enthusiasm for a journey into an attic. "I saw a light switch, some —" Boxes shifted from a pile and fell to the wood floor before Matt finished his thought. "You hurt, Peter?"

Instead of a reply, light flooded everything around them.

"I expected a solitary glass light bulb, but they went all out with the lights up here," Matt said.

"It's like broad daylight," Peter said and shuffled more boxes from his path.

"I found it. Our ship has come in," Victoria called out from the corner of the attic.

Scrambling feet found her fast. Victoria, Peter, and Matt stared at the large wooden box with two words painted on its side: MERRILL EMERSON.

Matt had never seen a smile from end to end on his mother's face as Victoria lifted the lid and directed a small flashlight at the treasures inside. The boy's mind whirled with all the possibilities hidden in a grand box. He'd seen his share of pirate movies and the gold that showed up along the way.

His mother pulled her arm out into the light.

"Papers?" Matt said with shock and equal parts disgust. Victoria brought the pile to her chest as if they were long-lost children and gazed at her find.

"What were you hoping for?" Peter asked his son.

"I don't know. Something more fun. More expensive," he admitted.

"I think the lost writings of spiritualist Merrill Emerson will be worth a lot of money," she said.

Peter reached into the wooden crate and plucked out something thin. "I think this might entertain you, my boy." He handed the artifact to Matt.

"What is it?" Matt studied the edges of the square piece of wood.

Peter laughed. "It's called a Ouija board."

"Peter, do you know the value of that? A Ouija owned by the inventor. What if it's his original—a prototype?" Victoria asked.

"Then I guess we're giving him his inheritance early," Peter said with a genuine smile.

Victoria shrugged and retreated to her documents. Matt gazed down at the smooth wood and the alphabet scrolled across its front.

"So, how does this thing work?" he asked Peter when they entered the boy's bedroom.

Peter placed the wooden board on the floor and studied the crudely carved slab of wood. "This thing is amazing. It looks like Tigerwood."

"What's that? I never heard of that type." Matt grabbed the board back and rubbed his hands across the surface.

"It's an exotic wood mostly found in South America. Brazil, I think. It grows where the land stays wet. I do know the wood is rare, though. Emerson was trying to do something special with this game."

"I don't understand."

"Instrument makers used this wood for the sound it conveys. They say it holds the spirits of the forest within its rings like a passenger. It has a fantastic shimmer, doesn't it?"

passenger

Matt nodded.

"The inventor reached out to the *beyond* with these things."

"Can we try it?" Matt asked with anticipation.

Peter shrugged, placed the wooden board on the floor, and crossed his legs in front of it.

"Here. Sit next to me. Your mom knows way more about this stuff than I do."

"What do we do?" Matt lifted a piece of wood; the end protruded like a finger.

"It's called a planchette."

"It looks more like a lemon. What do we do with it?"

"That, my boy, is our passage into…*the spirit world*," Peter said with a scary voice.

"Stop, Dad! Be serious."

"Oh. Pardon me." Peter sat up tall, pretending to straighten an invisible tie. "Let's begin then, good sir. Do you remember watching the movie *Gremlins*?"

"I loved it."

"As well you should. There were rules you must obey to own a gremlin—"

"Don't get them wet, no sunlight, and no food after midnight," Matt advised.

"Okay, smartie pants. The Ouija has its own set of rules that we must follow or *dire consequences will befall us all*," Peter announced in a creepy voice.

"Dad?"

"Sorry."

"What rules?" Matt asked with wide eyes.

"First, the lights must be off. No electronic devices allowed. They interfere with the spirits."

Matt turned the light switch down and sat in the dark as Peter lit a candle.

"Power off that laptop," Peter warned.

"It's dead," Matt promised. "What's next?"

"We rest our fingers on the planchette and the spirits will move it across the board for us. But only one of us can ask the questions. You want me to speak, or do you want to do it?"

"No way. Not me. Is it even safe?" Matt felt butterflies tickle his stomach

"Sure, it's safe. But never do this by yourself. And at the end, always say goodbye. To close the portal."

"What happens if we use this by ourselves?"

"I actually don't know. That's just what I've always heard." Peter laughed and Matt joined him. "Maybe we turn into spiders."

Matt's laughter died and he glared at Peter across the board, removing Peter's smile.

"So, here's how it goes." Peter moved the little plank in circles around the board. "This is how you warm it up or summon the spirits." As Peter moved faster and faster, Matt kept his eyes glued to the motion. "There, that should prime the pump full of apparitions." Peter saw his boy's wonder and smiled again. "Place your fingers lightly on the planchette."

Matt touched his fingertips onto the top side of the plank at the same time as his father.

"What do we say?"

Peter lifted his head toward the heavens. "Is there anyone here with us?" They turned their heads around them and watched the candlelight change every shadow into a creature. "Is someone in this room with us?" The candle flickered but stayed lit. "Are you a —" Their hands glided up to the top corner and stopped.

"It answered, yes," Matt said with trembling hands. "Ask it something else." The boy's eyes darted back and forth.

"Are there others with you?" The indicator moved to the other side.

"No," Matt spoke for the board.

"Can you tell us your name?"

Matt couldn't tell if it made circles—the movements were that fast. By the time he reached the second letter, he finally caught what it had spelled.

"M-E. His name is Me?" the boy asked.

"I don't think that's right," Peter said. Worry strained his voice.

"I'm sure of it, Dad."

Peter scanned the room and the shadows that danced. "How did you die?" Peter asked and stared at his son until Matt gave him a reassuring nod. The candle flickered harder than before and threatened to blow out, but somehow stayed lit. The planchette moved like it was on rails. "Are you doing that?" Peter asked.

Matt did nothing but shake his head. When their hands became still, they read the word: K-I-L-L-E-D.

"Killed? Someone killed you?" Their hands atop the wooden pointer moved smoothly from one letter to the next like a slithering creature.

"M-Y-S-E-L-F," Peter read and jerked the planchette over the black lettering of GOOD BYE at the bottom of the board. Matt's laptop sprung to life and lit the room with a flash. They stared at each other.

"I thought you said the battery was dead."

"It was. I swear." Matt focused on the board. "Didn't Grandpa take his own life?"

"I think I've had enough excitement for one night and it's getting late, don't you?" Peter scooped up the planchette, the board, and placed them on a closet shelf. "The Ouija board was used to scare people. There really is nothing else to it. It's just a fun way to put you on edge."

"I understand, Dad," Matt said with a hesitant smile.

"Sorry I introduced that to you so close to bedtime."

"I'm fine."

"Glad to hear it. Come say goodnight to Mom."

After his father left, Matt stared at the board, teetering on a shelf a while longer before he followed.

Scattered papers sat all around Victoria's bedroom when Matt and Peter entered. She couldn't contain her excitement and Matt felt the infectiousness of her mood. "It smells like the attic in here, Mom," he said, holding his nose.

Victoria gazed up and smiled. "Sorry. These things are a little musty. Upside? I hit the jackpot."

"How so?" Peter asked and sat on the one small space left empty on the bed. Some papers floated from off the bedspread to the floor below.

"It turns out that our friend Emerson *was* here in Ohio. Every second he spent in spiritualist camps is all documented in these papers."

"So did you find the connections between the mediums and how he created the Ouija board?" Peter asked.

Victoria stacked papers. "Not yet. But I will."

"I know you will."

Victoria let her hands fall onto his palm and squeezed. "I know this obsession has been hard. You both never complained about my long hours."

"I'm happy for you, Mom." Matt embraced her.

"Thank you," she said, close to tears.

"If you could see what we see, you wouldn't have to thank us. You did everything you said you would. I'm proud of you. Matt and I both are."

Victoria jumped onto Peter's lap and let herself cry into her husband's shoulder. The feeling was warm and way overdue.

Matt's bedroom sat in the center of the home. Not a single window to view the outside. Which also meant it was one of the darkest rooms in the house. A fact that didn't get past the teenager.

The dark terrified him as a child. Yet even now, he understood that getting older didn't mean your fears went away.

He had to learn, like everyone else, to tuck them down deep inside and pretend bravery. Matt's eyes flew open wide when a thud stirred him from sleep.

"Hello?" He recognized the fear in the one word he spoke. He leaned over the edge of his bed and saw the Ouija board at the bottom of his closet. Meagre light shone on the word YES.

He thought of his father's strange reaction to the game. *He's messing with me.* Still, the performance was the best he'd seen from him.

Without even knowing the *why* behind it, Matt glided to his closet and collected the board. He plopped his butt onto the end of his bed and leveled the board onto his knees.

"Alright, *Me.* Let's see what you have to say." Matt placed his hand on the planchette and watched it spin in circles just as his father did and closed his eyes tight.

"Are you near?" He sat there motionless for a long time. "Can you see me?"

A warming sensation passed through his fingertips. He almost jerked his hands away. Before he could, the wooden indicator moved across the board: YES.

He took a deep breath and continued. "Do you have something to tell me?" It never budged from its first answer. "Okay then. What do you want me to see?" He waited in his silent bedroom until the thing finally started its journey around the slick surface. When it was complete, he read the message aloud:

"Treasure Island." He withdrew his grasp, let his hands fall to his lap, and stared at the board. *Did I spell that without knowing?*

He shook his head and hoped the movement would jog a memory. Nothing came to mind.

He'd had the novel at some point. But he'd owned a hundred other books throughout his childhood, too.

And like kindling reacting to a spark, Matt stood up; recognition vibrated his body. He ran through the house, passing his parents having their morning coffee in the living room.

"Where are you going?" his mother called after him.

"I'm on a mission," he shouted and took the attic steps as if it were an Olympic event.

He remembered when they moved from their old home, they packed all their books inside their luggage. He thought it was a brilliant idea by his father and a much easier way to lug tons of books. But they had so many suitcases.

He unzipped the sides of the bags and poured through endless titles. He wasn't even sure if he still had the book, but he kept at it in the dusty attic. Matt coaxed books to the side, one after the other until his patience vanished and he resorted to tossing them away. With one suitcase left to search, Matt prepared himself for disappointment.

When he opened the leather flap, sitting right on top was a leather-bound edition of *Treasure Island* as if it were waiting for him all along. King Arthur finding Excalibur came to mind.

He pulled Robert Louis Stevenson's novel into his hand and stared at the cover in the dim light.

"Now what?" he spoke to himself. Turning the book over in his hands—he examined every detail. Nothing was out of place. Matt pulled the cover open and leafed through the pages.

A shimmer caught his eye, and he quickly shuffled until he saw what it was. He brought his hand to his mouth and felt tears trickle down his cheeks. His vision was blurry, but he couldn't stop them, no matter what.

From between the pages, he pulled a baseball card and brought it up to his face. The player on the card had a baseball bat propped on his shoulder as he gazed skyward.

"1952. Topps. Mickey Mantle," he spoke to himself, then stared at the last thing his grandfather ever gave him, letting the emotion take him over. "Why would I have put you in here? How could a board know this?"

The light was dim in his bedroom. Despite that, the Ouija board shimmered against the shag of his carpet. It wasn't just sitting there, a docile object; he would have sworn it breathed like a creature waiting for his return.

Matt folded his legs in front of the board and tried to remember the sound of his grandfather's voice. When he pressed fingers onto the indicator, a surge of energy warmed his fingertips.

"Grandpa?" he spoke to the board and heard the words echo in the empty room. He sat there for a long time, expecting a voice to speak back to him instead. *I guess it doesn't work that way.* With anticipation he couldn't resist, he placed his fingers on the wooden indicator. After a slide and a few circles, he repeated the question. A vibration started in his hands, and he doubted its existence a second before they flew to a word.

YES.

"I can feel you here, Grandpa." The planchette remained still. "Are you in pain where you are?" The indicator darted across the board.

NO.

Matt let out a breath and felt his lungs drain like a balloon. His thoughts whirled but landed on his next question. "Is there something I need to know?"

The indicator swirled around the center. D-A-N-G-E-R.

"Someone is going to hurt me?"

YES.

"Tell me what to do," Matt begged. Caught up in the moment, he nearly missed the first letter of the message.

F-I-N-D.

"What? Find what?" Panic strangled his tone.

T-A-C-K-L-E B-O-X. The words formed fast. O-N T-O-P. The last letter came into focus. Matt sprinted for the garage and toward the lone tackle box his family owned. In the garage's corner stood three fishing poles.

Two meant for his parents and one that belonged to him. They had gone fishing as a family once, that he remembered, and there they sat with a little green box resting underneath.

The way he approached the box appeared more like an explorer discovering an alien artifact or an officer deactivating a bomb. Anything but a boy reaching for a box full of hooks and lures. *Why would Grandpa lead me here?*

When he opened the lid, he found his answer gleaming *on top*, just as the board predicted. He watched the fluorescent light overhead shine down on the knife, accenting its deadly curves.

Plucking the tool and placing it into his hands, Matt felt a surge return like his interactions with the board. Although the knife was meant for cutting lines or fileting fish, the extreme curve of the blade radiated power.

After hours of talking to the board, then searching the house, he sat motionless in front of more objects his grandfather sent him to find. They made a unique shadow on the foot of his bed.

The wood handle of the knife sat in his palm like an extension of his hand. The power of a blade eluded him until that moment.

Along with the fishing knife, there was a yard of rope, a small fire extinguisher, a roll of quarters, a wooden chair from the dining room, and a bell. The items mesmerized him. A question tumbled through his mind. *What do I do with them now?* He asked the board a dozen times and, as active as it was when he retrieved the items, it was all but silent afterward.

"Thanks a lot, Grandpa." He stared at each thing until his eyes went blurry. "Maybe I'm doing something wrong." He was sure one person had the answers and if his mom couldn't help—no one could.

Victoria peeked over her books as she always did, but kept her attention buried in her work. Matt didn't take it personally anymore. There were one-sided conversations through the years, but he still loved her. That was her way.

"You know the years of you describing the spiritual things?" he asked, rubbing his hands together to occupy his mind.

"You mean your entire life?" Victoria asked without breaking eye contact from her book.

"Yeah. Those years." He found a bare spot on her bed and sat without toppling papers to the floor. "I need some info about Ouija boards."

Victoria did the unthinkable. She sat her book down and found her son's eyes. "Are you okay? You never ask me about spiritualism."

"Guess I'm overdue. Got a second?"

"Of course," she said with a smile that was slow to fade. Matt pressed a fist to his lips to hide his excitement. "Just ask me."

"How do Ouija boards work? Do they really work? If I contact someone, do I always get the same spirit? What about family? Are they attracted to the board?"

"Whoa. Slow down. Why the sudden interest in Ouija boards?"

"I knew you wouldn't help me—"

She grabbed his hand when he tried to get up.

"I'll help." When he sat down, they were quiet for a few moments. "Legend has it that the inventor Merrill Emerson created the Ouija board as a way of cheating death. He believed the boards to be a portal to return to life."

"That's not what I need, Mom," he said and slapped his knee.

"Then what?" she said in a quiet voice.

"Is it real? Can the spirits from the beyond contact us through it?" He watched her practice a speech before she let the words fall out.

"From what I've seen…yes. But people with the ability to channel a spirit with a board…" She paused. "They're like a grain of sand in a desert. It's not even worth mentioning the number—it's that small."

"Then how do you know it's possible?" he asked and wrung his hands.

"Because I became a grain of sand." Victoria smiled. "That's right. I got a Ouija board when I was a teenager and talked to spirits. And it scared the hell out of me. I thought everyone could do it. I found out I was not like everyone else."

"What happened?"

"It was like the real world. You never know who's on the other side of a door. A spirit deceived me."

"Are they all bad? The ones that come through?"

Victoria shook and wouldn't look away.

"No. But the odds are against you finding a good one. That's why I never used a board again. The fascination for the phenomenon never left me, but I directed my energy to the science *behind* spiritualism," she said and laughed. "I know. I sound ridiculous using the word science next to spiritualism. But there's a connection there. I'm sure of it."

"I understand."

"Have you used a Ouija board by yourself?" she asked.

"No. Never," he lied. Victoria let out a sigh. "I was just curious," he added.

"Good. They aren't toys. We can't believe everything *Hasbro* says," she said with a smile returning.

"Back when you used the board…what did you do wrong?" Matt moved closer to his mom, and she moved back. Her expression lost all humor.

"I didn't say goodbye. It allows the spirit into your home for as long as you leave the door open. I awoke something dangerous."

"But what if you need to leave the connection open?" Matt asked.

"Why would you need to stay connected to something dead?"

"I wouldn't. You wouldn't. It just popped into my head. That's all," he said.

"Always say goodbye," she said, her eyes fixed on his.

Matt sat in his bedroom and watched the fading sunlight stream through the glass of his window. For hours he had tried to reach his grandfather, and every attempt failed except one word: TONIGHT.

Until that week, Matt wasn't in touch with how much he missed his grandfather. He was always there for him. School lunches, choir recitals, and every holiday meant his grandpa would be there to share the memories. He had taken those precious moments for granted. He wasn't just a family member, but the glue that held their family close. His grandfather traveled across time and space for *him*.

The fear of an intruder hurting him, or his parents, was more than he could stand. But trying to unravel the mystery items to save their lives sent a chill through his skin.

The bell was straight forward, or at least that's what he thought when he placed it in the hallway that led to his parent's bedroom.

As soon as everyone was asleep and the house went quiet, he tied a string to the bell and extended both sides to the wall—duct tape held it all together.

He'd seen *The Goonies* enough times to realize he needed to hear the intruder coming. A booby trap was his answer. The other things he collected were a riddle he hoped he could solve.

He sat in his dark bedroom, Ouija board by his side, the small fire extinguisher in his left hand, and the fishing knife in the right.

The Rock'em Sock'em Robots that he had as a kid came into his mind. *I hope I can keep my head on my shoulders.* The urge to start another session with his grandfather took hold.

The board was just sitting there, waiting for someone to talk to it. And he needed more help. *One quick chat.*

When he put the knife down to touch the planchette, a bell rang from the hall. The high chime made him sit up straight before he bounded to his feet. His bedroom door wasn't open, but he stared at the wood grains for signs of life, anyway. Waiting for another chime. And then it dawned on him—the intruder wasn't heading into *his* room. As the pieces all came together, his mother screamed.

Twisting the knob, he swung open the door and rushed to his parent's room. All his fear forgotten. An urgency took its place. Their bedroom door—closed tight hours before, sat wide open like a hungry mouth, waiting for him to step inside. His mother wasn't screaming any longer, but he could hear her begging as Matt entered.

As his eyes adjusted, everything inside was shades of black and gray.

"Please don't hurt him," his mom whispered. As Matt crept closer to their bed, the shapes came into focus, and he saw a stranger straddling his father. Pressed into a corner, shaking from sobs, was his mother.

"Hey, you!" Matt said in his most authoritative tone. The intruder flinched. When the shadowy figure turned, half of his frame was on his father and half slid off the bed. And that's when Matt saw a blade stuck in the meat of his father's shoulder. The urge to vomit bubbled in his throat. It wasn't the sight of a knife deep in his father. That *was* a horror, but when he remembered he put his knife down next to the Ouija board, he wanted to scream.

With the intruder frozen in place and the fishing knife useless in another room, he lifted the fire extinguisher and blasted it onto the stranger. Cold white foam covered the face and body of the man. At first, no one moved. Even his mother went silent as the layer of white blanketed her husband's assailant. Matt took a slow step backward, aware somehow that the extinguisher had enraged his opponent.

The intruder pulled the knife from his father and scrambled off the bed. The teenager opened the valve of the extinguisher. Foam exploded into the stranger's face as he backed away to his own room. The distraction worked—guiding danger away from his parents, but if he didn't produce a plan fast, it was all for nothing. His first sight when he entered his room was the items circling the board. From instinct, Matt grabbed the dining room chair and turned it in time as the man entered. He imagined he appeared as a lion tamer as he used the chair. Still wiping away foam, the man missed the outstretched chair as Matt drove him back toward the wall.

The legs of the chair knocked against the drywall while the leg spindles slammed into his opponent's throat. The gargled gasp coming from the grizzly man gave him satisfaction, but soon his advantage was all but gone.

Matt had the chair one second, the next second, snatched from his hands, and tossed to the side. Falling back toward the bed and his magical objects, he grabbed at the knife with one hand and a roll of quarters with the other.

The thought of stabbing someone, even if they threatened his family, was a scary choice. Instead, he darted the knife out and made his adversary shift. Matt hurled his fist toward the man's jaw. Even without the strength of a full-grown man, the impact of the punch, curled around the solid roll of quarters, rocked the intruder back onto stumbling feet.

The man let out a growl and charged the boy with the point of a tactical knife. Matt caught his arm in time, but because he was smaller he became a passenger. All he could do was slide back and let the full weight of his enemy fall onto him, feeling the thud of his floor. *This is the end.*

The intruder pulled back and lunged for Matt's chest. With the reflexes a child possessed, Matt grabbed the Ouija board and held it out for defense. The tip of the blade slid into the wood.

His fishing knife sat next to him, but felt a million miles away. *Should I try for the knife?*

The attacker's blade protruded from the word: YES.

That was all the answer he needed. As the stranger pulled his weapon free from the board, Matt reached for the knife, thrust it forward, and found the softness of a belly.

His rival groaned and collapsed backward, clutching his wrecked stomach.

Nimble fingers found the yard of rope and secured the hands behind his back as tight as he could manage.

Flashing blue and red lights flooded the hallway—officers bustled through the house as EMTs secured his father onto a rolling gurney.

"I'm okay," Peter spoke to comfort his son. "Thanks to you."

Matt hugged his father tight and buried himself into his arms. Tears fell as they wheeled the gurney toward the door.

"I'll meet you at the hospital," Victoria called after Peter, then turned to Matt. "An officer will stay here with you when I go with your dad. Okay?"

"Okay."

"How did you stop him? How'd you expect this?" Victoria asked.

After a moment of hesitation, Matt spoke. "It was Grandpa. He spoke to me through the Ouija board."

Victoria gave him a puzzled smile.

"I guess I'm a grain of sand in the desert, just like you. And not all spirits are bad," he added.

Victoria revealed a genuine smile and tilted her head up toward the ceiling.

"You saved my family," she spoke to the wind. "You're welcome to anything in the house." Victoria hugged her son. "I'm going to get dressed and I will check in on you before I leave."

Walking back to his bedroom, Matt felt special for the first time in his life and thankful his grandpa had never left his side.

Matt stood in his room and marveled at everything he had done that night. He never believed in the spiritual world. It was always like stories of hucksters taking advantage of the weak-minded. Now, touched by something greater than himself, he saw a whole new world revealed. He turned the board over and made a circle to start the session.

"Thank you, Grandpa. For everything."

M-E.

"I know you, Grandpa."

NO. The indicator darted around the board in furious motions. M-E-R-R-I-L-L E-M-E-R-S-O-N. All at once, Matt understood. The spirit speaking through the board was never his grandfather. M-O-M W-A-S R-I-G-H-T. Matt mouthed the words. A-L-W-A-Y-S S-A-Y— Matt watched the word at the bottom of the board: GOOD BYE.

Before he could sign off, a flash of white pierced his eyes and threw him to the floor. With a quick head shake, pulling himself to a sitting position, Merrill placed *his* new hands on the indicator.

"Are you there?"

YES.

"I'm sorry it had to be you."

W-H-Y? Matt asked.

"Because I wanted out, and I needed a vessel," Merrill said as he slid the planchette to the words GOOD BYE—closing the portal. The door opened from behind.

"Are you okay, Matt?" Victoria asked.

"I'm fine…now."

"Is Grandfather still here?"

Merrill shook his head and tucked the Ouija board under his arm before sliding it onto the shelf of his closet and placed a book on top of it. "That other person went away. It's *just* me now."

Victoria smiled, and Merrill smiled back.

~ THE KEEPSAKE ~

Everything about Rachel was mesmerizing. Marie stared at her stepsister for a long time. The way she spoke with her hands or flipped her hair off her face seemed picture perfect to a girl who never got attention from those around her. Even the way Rachel took bird-size bites of her breakfast fascinated her.

"Are you two adjusting?" Andrew spoke to his daughter Marie but gave Rachel a side glance to show he meant it for both.

"We're doing great," Rachel said, showing all her teeth. "I was nervous about sharing a new home, but you and Marie have been so welcoming."

Melanie slid under Andrew's arm and squeezed him tight.

"They have been great. I have no reason to try and take over the role of a mother. I hear she was wonderful. I just want us to be friends. Okay?" Melanie asked.

"I want that too," Marie said and chose her words carefully. She felt a twinge when the subject of her mother came up.

"What was your mother like?" Rachel blurted.

When Marie lowered her head, Andrew stepped closer. "She was an amazing woman." Andrew pumped his daughter's arm.

"Tell us something interesting about her," Melanie prodded. Andrew rocked in place until an answer arrived.

"Marie's mom, Angela, was a practicing witch," Andrew said. Everyone looked around for a reaction.

"Wait. You're serious?" Rachel asked and clapped her hands with anticipation.

"Not really. My dad is exaggerating."

"Not one bit. She studied the natural world as well as witchcraft and the shadow that surrounds it. In fact, just before her passing, she sat Marie down and promised her that she would protect her from the grave."

"You never told me this, Andrew. Are you pulling our legs?" Melanie asked.

"Yeah. That part's true. She even had a keepsake box that she kept for spells and curses," Marie said.

"Oh my God! Shut up! Can I see the box?" Rachel asked. Marie had never seen eyes so wide.

"It's gone," Marie said and lowered her head once more. Marie read the disappointment in her stepsister's face.

"It was her final wish for the box to be buried with her," Andrew whispered as if Marie wasn't in the room.

"That's a shame. That would have been cool as hell."

"Rachel," Melanie scolded. "I'm so sorry about that."

"No. it would have been cool," Marie said and tried to read Rachel's expression as the parents walked away.

When footsteps faded out of the room, Rachel's smile vanished.

"Listen to me."

Marie recognized Rachel's intensity and made a fist to calm her nerves.

"My mother and I have done fine without anyone. If you try to suck up all my mom's attention, I will make your ass pay. Are you hearing me?" Rachel pushed her nose onto Marie's.

A weak nod was all Rachel got back.

"Growing pains," was what her dad told her.

Marie wished it was that simple.

No matter what she did, Rachel never gave her a chance to be friends. If Marie spoke too long during dinner or spoke at all some nights, Rachel would glare at her the entire meal. *What does she want from me?*

Marie didn't want a stepmother, but even further down the list was a stepsister like Rachel. She was just figuring out how to talk to boys—sort of. She'd worked past a shyness that had plagued her for as long as she could remember.

No sooner had she unraveled the mysteries of her world without a mother, when a blue-eyed, blonde-haired demon moved into her home and pushed away her comfort.

The demon called herself Rachel. Her eyes were bright. Clear skin, and a bubbly personality.

Worst of all, Rachel was the most beautiful girl Marie had ever seen. *What does that make me? The ugly stepsister?*

Marie saw through her act even if her father couldn't. Around the adults, Rachel was sweet and a doting sister, but her façade snapped the moment she knew she was alone. She couldn't live like an outsider in her home any longer. *Go put her on the defensive. See how she likes it.*

"You don't eat much, do you?" Marie directed the question to her sister at the dinner table. Rachel sat higher in her chair—easily a foot taller than Marie. That was a first for her and Marie wanted to smile but contained the inbound smirk.

"My mom always taught me *we,* as humans, don't need as much food as we think," Rachel said, leaning forward, and grabbing her mom's hand. "Right, Mom?"

Melanie shifted from her newspaper and threw her daughter a smile.

"Absolutely," Melanie agreed, and was back to her paper. Marie knew Melanie wasn't listening but saw Rachel's satisfied look anyway.

"I guess your mom never had time to teach you that before she died. Marie, I promise you. If you eat less, your stomach will shrink and so will your waistline."

Marie stared at Rachel in disbelief. She swiveled her head to her father and stepmother.

"My parents taught me that beauty is on the inside. Right, Dad?"

Andrew never looked Marie's way. No reaction at all.

With a book propped on her knee, Marie leaned into her chair and let her mind fall into the novel. The story so captured her attention, she never heard Rachel walk into the room or slide into a seat next to her.

"You're not a hopeless case." Rachel broke the silence and caused Marie to drop her book.

"What are you saying?"

"That you aren't undatable."

"I never thought I was," Marie said, anger seeping out of every syllable.

"I have the perfect guy for you," she said with too much enthusiasm.

"You just moved to our town. How could you know anybody yet?" Even as she asked, Marie knew the answer. With Rachel's attractiveness, she never worked for anything.

"Honestly, he's the brother of the guy I'm interested in." Rachel dug into her purse, brought out makeup, and applied some to her face. *So unnecessary.*

"Thanks for thinking of me, but—"

"No, really. You'd be doing me a favor. Guys always want to move fast when they meet me and with another couple, it will make it light and fun," she promised.

"I don't know."

Rachel took Marie by both hands and squeezed her palms.

"Trust me, it'll be a blast. Besides, I've seen Kyle's brother. Cute."

Marie had no answer, but she wanted to meet a boy.

"Okay," Marie relented. "Let's do it," she said with a smile, letting the words burst from her with excitement.

"Tomorrow then. I will set it up." Rachel shook her arms with excitement and headed out of the room. Did her father say something to Rachel? Why was she being so nice? She'd never shown any kindness before.

Whatever the reason, Marie was happy her stepsister was trying. Her eyes landed on the empty rocking chair that belonged to her mother and thought she saw it move.

Marie and Rachel sat next to each other in the restaurant with sports souvenirs surrounding them on the walls.

They offered glances, but had nothing to say. Marie finally thought of something.

"What do you think of my dress?" Marie asked. "It was my mother's spring dress."

Rachel watched her phone a moment longer before regarding the question.

"Oh yeah. It's something," she said with her attention still on her phone. Marie saw the shadow from the glowing device. *You don't know a thing about me.*

"My mother wore this when she met my father." Marie straightened the dress. "It's so white that I don't dare wear it. It just felt like the right occasion."

"That's a great story," Rachel said and returned to her phone.

Marie shook off the doubt and widened her smile when she saw two boys head their way.

For all the talk of how *Kyle* would move too fast, she saw Rachel pull him close and plunge her tongue into his mouth. As they made a scene, Marie got a glimpse of Patrick. The younger of the brothers never looked her way. His head was down until he found a chair around the table.

When Rachel pulled herself away—wiping her mouth off—

Kyle took a sip of a cherry slushie he brought with him and stared at Marie sitting across from each other in silence.

"Well. Look at you two," she said and sat in Kyle's lap.

"They are natural together," Kyle added.

"Patrick? This is Marie," Kyle encouraged.

As Patrick sat, his cute smile drew her.

"Hello," Patrick said. "You're Rachel's sister? She looks nothing like you."

Marie fell inside herself with her vision narrowing to a tunnel in front of her. She shifted her eyes to Rachel, who tilted her head before showing a grin wider than she ever saw on her.

As the moments passed, recognition swept over her. They opened the menu but shared glances back and forth. They were laughing at her.

"Aren't you going to say something back to Patrick? Like how great he looks?" Rachel blinked her eyelids fast to emphasize her question.

"Hey Patrick," Marie said and tried to read the teenager's expression. "Do you date a lot?"

"Way more than you, I'm sure," Patrick said and returned to his menu.

Rachel broke out into laughter from the comment and Marie didn't want to speak anymore.

After a long time of silence, Rachel cupped her hands around her mouth and whispered into Kyle's ear. He smiled bright before they returned to the menu.

"Hey Kyle, isn't Marie's dress pretty?"

"It is pretty."

"It's an heirloom," Rachel said.

"Marie, wanna try some of my slushie? It's cherry."

Before Marie could refuse, Kyle splashed the contents of the melting drink all over her. Red drink soaked her white dress until her upper half was the color of crimson. Marie looked down at her mother's dress in horror.

"It's just red dye number 5. I'm sure it will come out," Kyle said with a smile. They all began to laugh with Rachel standing out as the hardest.

When Marie got to her feet, the juice from the slushie ran down to the bottom of her dress.

Rachel and Kyle grinned furiously as she dripped. Marie stood awkwardly in place as a waiter fetched her napkins.

"That was totally my fault. Send me the cleaning bill." The comment brought more laughs with Patrick joining this time. Patrick was the last straw. With tears rolling down her cheeks, Marie ran for the door.

The walk home from the restaurant was a blur of anger. Marie thought about her mother and how the night wouldn't have happened if she were still alive.

She slipped quietly into the house, removed her stained dress, and covered herself with a robe two sizes too big. Rachel made her feel small, and she wanted to keep feeling that way. Like listening to sad music when you were already sad, she embraced the pain her stepsister caused her.

Marie settled into the family den, which had always been her reading nook, with her thoughts drifting to her mother's keepsake box. How she wished she still had it.

It was an abstract idea, and she didn't even know what she would've done with its contents. Still, there was power within it she wanted more than anything.

She remembered her mother's journals radiating power, but she also felt the potential for darkness. *Why would Rachel do that to me?*

"You are rude as hell," Rachel said as she entered the den.

A fire that consumed her hours before ignited once more in Marie, warming her face.

"You destroyed my mother's dress," she spoke in a whisper.

"It was a joke. What, you can't take a prank?"

"You are hateful," Marie said through clenched teeth.

"And you're a sad girl clinging to a dead mother."

"Look at you with your blonde hair, manicured nails, designer clothes. And you're passing judgment on me?"

"At least I'm not invisible, like you."

Rachel shifted away for the first time. When she turned back, hatred had transformed Marie's face. The truth doused Marie like a plunge into cold water.

"You humiliated me." Marie walked closer. Behind her a rocking chair began to move.

Rachel pointed toward the swinging.

"The rocking chair is—"

"Shut up!" Marie dug her nails into her palms. "You bragged about your mother and what she taught you." The rocking chair rocked faster, and swayed like a pendulum. "My mother taught me things, too. My mother came from the old country and what she knew was ancient."

Rachel watched the rocker as it swung violently into place behind Marie.

"Why are you telling me this?" Rachel asked, fear muffling the words.

"Because you're a bad person."

Rachel shook her head and watched the rocking chair with wide eyes.

"No. I'm not. Listen, Marie—" Rachel's body heaved forward, and she grabbed her stomach as if punched.

"I hate you," Marie said before walking away.

Rachel fell to her knees and clutched her belly. She watched the tempo of the chair slow and with it, the intensity of her pain.

When morning light hit Rachel's eyes, she remembered her stomach. She'd spent the night doing everything she could to make her suffering go away. Late into the night, it finally did.

Exhausted, she drifted off, but not before she thought of Marie and the rocking chair. *Was it all in my mind?*

She lifted herself to a sitting position against her headboard and felt the tenderness under her belly button. *That sure is real.* Marie was a pushover. That's what she thought when she first met her stepsister.

Brushing her long blonde hair off her face, sliding the duvet to the side, and swinging her feet to the floor, she froze in place. On the nightstand, next to her bed, sat a bouquet of freshly cut flowers. What struck her was the color. The tulips were the brightest yellow she'd ever seen.

Somehow, the vase full of flowers had appeared magically by her side while she slept, and she noticed no one coming or going. *Marie!* It was the logical explanation. *The guilt of hurting me. She tried to make up for it. There was no way a rocking chair caused that pain, and you know it.* Either way, the flowers were her way of apologizing, and that satisfied her.

When Rachel saw her stepsister in the hall, she stopped her.

"Thank you."

"For what?" Marie asked, not making eye contact.

"The flowers. They're beautiful."

Marie acted as if she hadn't a clue what she was talking about but nodded and walked away.

"Weirdo," Rachel whispered and headed for the bathroom. Walking past her mother and stepfather's room, she saw her mother moving frantically in circles.

Rachel couldn't resist the temptation and moved slowly to their door.

"It's not working with the girls," her mother said.

"We have to be patient," her stepfather assured. "These things take time."

Rachel's skin crawled when she heard them speaking about her. But a part of her wanted to fix the situation with Marie for her mother.

Putting the ugliness with Marie behind, Rachel wanted an outfit to match the flowers. She chose an orange dress—a burst of color like the sun. She slid one of the freshly snipped yellow flowers behind an ear.

In the school hallway, teenagers bustled past Rachel in every direction. They reminded her of ants pushing food back and forth instead of students preparing for school.

It was the back of Kyle's school jacket she saw first. He leaned against his locker. When she spotted him, her heart skipped a beat. Feeling the yellow flower balanced on her ear, she widened her smile as she approached him with excitement.

"Hey, cutie," she said and ran a hand down his back across the school mascot embroidered on his jacket. He swiveled around with surprise on his face that was slow to go away. Next to him was another girl, the opposite of her—black hair and curvy.

"Rachel?"

"Who's this?" she asked and studied the girl in tight clothes. Before Kyle answered, the girl scrambled away. He looked back, and they shared a glance that made Rachel feel worse.

"She's—"

"Don't lie to me."

"An improvement," he said with a smile.

The air went out of her chest, and she felt the flower twitch behind her ear.

"What the hell is wrong with you?" The yellow flower head convulsed again.

"We done now?" Kyle asked.

"Yeah. We're done," Rachel said.

Kyle edged away from the locker. The flower mirrored his movement and leaned to Rachel's right, but remained perched on her ear. He continued to speak, but his voice fell into the background.

Out of the corner of her eyes, she watched the flower shift with Kyle. Rachel lifted her hand and waved goodbye to Kyle as if to say go. The gesture got the response she wanted.

"Screw you!" he said and walked away.

With a steady hand, she reached her fingers out toward the animated flower and pulled it in front of her face. It was as lifeless as when she cut it down to size that morning. *I'm going crazy.*

She pushed it close to her nose to breathe in its fragrance, and that's when it came alive. The petals changed into an angry mouth, snapping at her face.

"What the hell?" The flower yanked its body in her direction, still chomping. Rachel brought her hands around the flower and felt a sting. When she withdrew a hand, it was dripping with blood. "You bastard!"

Stiffening its frame, the plant extended the mouth onto Rachel's neck and dug sharp teeth into her She screamed as it burrowed into her skin, undulating further inside. Half in with the bottom of a stem dangling, she pawed at her neck. With each attempt, the flower squirmed from her grasp. Her eyes opened wide when she felt the thing chewing.

In one violent motion, her hand connected with the writhing stem and slid it from her skin. The sound of the animated plant dragging from her neck was slimy. The noise reminded her of a leach, and she nearly puked when she saw the blood-covered creature in daylight.

Wrapping it in her hands, Rachel squeezed it with all her strength. In horror, she heard it scream and watched it fall to the floor.

With its half-crushed body, it heaved like a worm and released a shriek. Rachel used her boot to stop its movement for the last time. She stood there questioning whether the scene happened at all.

Slamming her bedroom door wide open, Rachel stared at the yellow flowers swaying in their vase like serpents. Rage filled her with every step toward them.

She grasped the stems of all the flowers at once and gripped them as tight as she could. She broke into a run, sliding Marie's door open, and moved to Marie resting on her bed.

"What the hell are you—"

Rachel tilted the flowers into her stepsister's face. The hungry mouths of the flowers clenched their teeth and extended themselves to get Marie.

"Did your mother do this?" Rachel asked and pushed the flowers even closer before tossing them onto the bed. Heading for the door, she turned back in time to see Marie batting and slamming the flowers in a panic.

"Be careful. They're from the old country."

Falling asleep had taken Marie a lot longer than usual, and Rachel was the reason. Except in the hall that morning, they hadn't said a word to each other.

Her stepsister weaved in and out of her dreams the entire night until a sound drew her from sleep. The noise was metallic, metal scraping against metal. As slumber threatened to take her back under, her eyes popped open with fear. Her mind tried to connect the noise, but nothing concrete came to her until she twisted her head toward her pillow.

Resting on the edge of her bed was a silver pair of scissors. Finding a sharp tool so close to her head frightened her. *How did you get there?*

She was a light sleeper, always had been. Somebody had come inside her room and left the shears without so much as a sound. *Except there was a cutting sound.*

Marie jolted to a sitting position and searched for movement in her bedroom, sure someone was hiding. There wasn't a way to get out so fast. *How long was I asleep?*

She brought her hand up to her chest and felt her breathing constrict.

She saw something she hadn't noticed before in the dim light. *A snake or a worm?*

When she moved her face closer, the object wasn't alive, didn't squirm or move at all.

Curiosity won out, and she picked up the object resting next to the scissors. It was hair, her hair. Someone had cut a long strand of her brown hair and left it next to her pillow.

Marie touched the side of her head and found where it came from. *It's Tuesday! How could Rachel know about Tuesdays?* Marie scrambled from her bed to her closet and ignored the obstacles as best she could in the dark and ran to find her father.

When she found him he was already heading for his car.

"Dad?" she said, close to tears.

Andrew spun on his heels to face his daughter.

"I'm late, what's up?"

"What did you tell Rachel about Mom's box?"

"What do you mean?"

Marie held out her hand with a strand of hair scissors.

"It's a curse to cut your hair on Tuesdays. Rachel discovered the curse. She has the box."

"That's impossible. It's safely with your mother. Maybe you did it in your sleep," Andrew said and pulled Marie close for a hug.

Marie pulled hard from his grasp.

"What are you talking about? Rachel did this to me."

Andrew shook his head.

"No, she didn't. Listen, we'll talk about this tonight when I get home."

Marie started to cry and rushed away from her father and back inside.

Rachel was already off to school before Marie could confront her. Every step into school was like waiting for an accident to happen. Cutting your hair on a Tuesday was a bad idea and one of the first things her mother taught her as a child. It should've been easy enough to prevent, except she never expected someone to creep into her room and cut it. She had misjudged Rachel, but she would not let that happen ever again.

Marie stared at her scalpel in science class for a long time. Her mother never told her what exactly would happen to her if she cut her hair on a Tuesday, but considering it took sharp scissors to start the curse, dissecting a frog made her wary.

She held the surgical tool close to the skin of the frog but gripped it tight so it couldn't fall from her hand or bounce off the classroom table and pierce an eye. Instead of all the fancy Final Destination dramatic outcomes, the blade cut the frog's skin. That was it. Marie exhaled pent-up air. Her lab partner regarded her like she was crazy. *If you only knew the truth.*

Before her nerves settled, a sound filled the classroom. The noise woke up something she didn't even remember consciously, but the part of her that awakened that morning recognized it at once. It was the snipping of the scissors.

It was a metal against metal whipping sound that kept a rhythmic pace. She grabbed the place where she lost a strand of hair and twirled it around her finger. The act was her way of soothing her nerves.

The sound had to be coming from inside herself. Others in the room turned around, looking for the source of the sound.

All eyes tilted upward, and she followed their glances to an industrial ceiling fan high above them.

"Shit," she said as the wobbling fan made a snapping noise with the blades breaking free. The surrounding kids screamed, but those voices were far away. Insignificant. She predicted where the spinning blade would end up.

The steel edge of the fan's blade twirled in circles, then sliced through Marie's lower stomach, and ended its journey in the school table. *How could a superficial girl like Rachel put a curse on me?* Her insides slid from the gaping wound. She watched her classmates push her intestines back into the folds of her belly.

Rachel couldn't stop crying as her mother wrapped her arms around her. Her stepfather joined in the hug.

"I'm so sorry for Marie," Rachel said between sobs. "Why did this happen?"

Andrew pulled away with a lost expression.

"Marie's a fighter. She's coming home to us," Andrew said.

"Did you see her in the hospital? Were you even there? Something evil caused that," Rachel shouted.

"It was just an accident," Melanie said and went in for another hug.

"How could you call that an accident? The things that happened to me, she went through too," Rachel shouted and pulled away like her mother was pulsating with live wires.

"I know it doesn't make sense. It all will in time," her mother assured.

"You're not hearing me." She scowled at both adults. "Marie's mother wants to kill us."

Melanie tried to hug her daughter once more, but this time Rachel flung her arms away.

"It's all in your head," Andrew said.

"I'm next," Rachel said, peering into her mom's eyes. "You know that, right?" Rachel walked out of the room.

Andrew tried on a smile for Melanie before moving to their closet. He pulled down the keepsake box from a shelf and slid out the journals and handwritten notes.

"Our work isn't done yet," Andrew said with a serious expression. Melanie nodded. He rifled through the journal of curses and stopped. "This is the one."

"Are you sure?" she asked. "The rocking chair didn't and neither did the flowers."

"Her mother and I learned these together. A chain letter will do the trick. Trust me. You write it and I will place it under Rachel's pillow."

She flashed him an expression that made him take a step back.

"I followed through with *my* child. Now you do yours. If we see this through to the end, we'll soon be free of them," Andrew said.

~ WHISPERS FROM THE CELLAR ~

The moving truck wasn't even half empty when Tabitha's stuffed animals found their spot in her bedroom. Bears, a dolphin, and other creatures stared back at her from every flat surface in the room. She fiddled with a silver bracelet, the words *Daddy Loves You* etched onto the front.

Most girls, by their ninth year, had plenty of stuffies. But there was a special hold a creature had over Tabitha. She couldn't explain her love for animals. Even at an early age, she already liked them much more than people.

As the movers bustled around her new home, she arranged her plushies in action scenes that made them appear as if they would come alive to dance around the room. She wanted them to breathe, to cuddle up, and nuzzle their noses into hers.

A dog was what she wanted. But Eli, her stepfather, said his allergies were way too bad for a pet. Begging for a dog, followed by a cat, then a hamster, all failed. That's when her number of stuffed animals got out of control. Even her mom said so.

The idea of having a stepfather was strange. One second it was just her and her mom, and the next she had to act like she had a new family. "What are you doing in here?" A voice broke Tabitha from her concentration. "Why aren't you helping us? It seems like half this shit is yours," Eli shouted in her tiny bedroom. He didn't belong in her room, and she felt weird inside when he decided to enter.

"I was…sorry, Eli."

"Dad. You are to call me *Dad*," he said, putting on a manufactured smile.

The word alone conjured up images of her father in a hospital bed. She had spent the last year trying not to use the word after her father died. And now a man she hardly spent time with wanted her to say it twenty times a day for the rest of her life.

"I'll help…Dad." The words slid out as solid as cranberry sauce from a can.

Eli smoothed out his black, greasy hair. His expression went blank.

"Good. Because your mother and I sure as hell ain't doing it all."

Tabitha had seen Eli crouched in a corner drinking his beer all day. She wasn't sure why he was so mad at *her*.

When Eli shuffled out of her bedroom, her father's last bed at the hospital sprang into her head. It was her father's skin that wasn't like skin anymore. See-through. The memory caused her to shiver.

Eli was gone, but his aftershave stayed behind to keep her company. Her nose guided her to the empty doorway, and she noticed another door directly in front of hers.

Her mother told her that old houses were set up differently than modern ones. A hundred years ago, owners had different needs. She didn't understand what she meant, except that they arranged rooms in strange ways. The hallways made a circle around the staircase that led up. Her feet carried her forward to the door with the words tumbling around in her mind.

The door across the hallway was exactly like hers. Same carved molding—same wooden front, and the same brass doorknob. What drew her attention was the old keyhole. It wasn't like anything she'd ever seen before. The place a key slid in was like a hungry mouth ready to chomp. Unable to resist, Tabitha extended her fingers to the handle until her palm rested on its smooth surface.

The metal was warm, like an object too close to a campfire. The warming continued when she curled her fingers around the knob. With a twist, she felt it turn back. Someone fought to keep it closed on the other side. She had little strength, but she used all she had to rotate the handle. It spun back, sending a chill down her spine.

Tabitha pulled herself from the door and went down on all fours to study the keyhole at eye level. A flicker of red sent her scrambling. Hunched over as if she were a dog—she kept eye contact with the keyhole but shuffled back to the safety of her room.

That night, Tabitha's mom kissed her on her cheek and, without warning, headed back towards the bedroom door. She'd always read Tabitha a book and cuddled on her bed before she met Eli. Just the two of them talking about their day—their quiet time. But it happened less and less. There was a desperation to keep her mom close. "Do you like our new home, Mom?"

"I do." Nikki flashed her daughter a smile. "It must be strange to share a new house after your dad left us. Do you want to talk about it?"

Tabitha turned her head toward the wall and shook her head hard. The tears were already on their way.

"It's important that we talk about your father. You can't keep things inside."

Nikki stared at her daughter a long time before she tucked the covers around her and made her way out of the child's bedroom.

With her mother halfway out the door, Tabitha gave into her panic. The talk about her dad ruined everything and she didn't want to let another night go without their *special time*.

"Mom? Can you—"

Eli appeared behind Tabitha's mother, wrapping her into his arms and giving her a long kiss.

"Let me say goodnight to her, Nikki. You go get ready for bed," Eli said, with an odd expression. Her mom smiled at him and left without a glance back at her.

Eli watched his wife disappear into another part of the house before his attention finally fell back onto Tabitha. She clutched her bedspread tight when he made his way to her bed, plopping onto the edge of the mattress.

"You didn't help much today, but thank you for trying," he said, studying her bedroom. "You were the one who had time to unpack their room. Good for you." He presented his words with a smile.

She wasn't sure he was being nice or not, so she smiled back.

"I know you're just a kid. It might be hard for you to understand," he said, leaning closer to Tabitha's face, "but the first months of a marriage are the most important. Critical really."

Tabitha *didn't* understand.

"You've had a lot of years with Nikki, so let's not be selfish, Okay?" Eli nodded, so Tabitha nodded back. "What I'm saying is you need to expect less time with your mom now that I'm here."

"Less?" she asked in a small voice.

Eli's nod returned.

"I want you to think of yourself as a silent partner."

She was still confused.

"No more asking for bedtime stories. That's my time with her."

"But she's my mom—"

Eli swung his arm fast. The sound of the slap, meaty and solid, was as bad as the searing pain it delivered. Almost. Eli placed his hand back to his side as Tabitha's eyes went wide with surprise and filled with tears.

"When I was a kid, I had a dog that took advantage of me. Begging for food, always trying to suck up the attention from my parents. But it learned fast and so will you."

They sat there in the quiet until Tabitha finally got the courage to speak.

"But your allergies. How did you have a dog?" she asked. The smack came faster than before.

"Now you're learning," he said. "Nighty night."

She didn't dare speak again. Tabitha bit her lip and watched him flip the lights off. He left the same way he arrived—like a tornado. She couldn't stop the tears after that. She let the sadness wash over her and wondered what her mom would say to Eli if she ever found out he hit her.

Her vision adjusted to the darkness as she listened to the faint sound of the grown-ups as they talked in another part of the old house. She saw the cellar door directly in front of her across the hallway. Remembering the door handle made her heart race and, as if by thinking of it alone, the knob jiggled.

The door created a loud clack as it swung open. Her arm tingled as her hair stood on end. Even as her chest tightened from the noise, curiosity told her to see who made the sound.

The door kept creaking and curiosity evaporated like water turning to steam. Although the urge to pull the covers over her head was strong, she couldn't take the chance. Whatever came from the cellar would see her in the dark.

A scratching across the wood floor came first. Something heavy scraped against the surface and came through her doorway. She was a mouse afraid of a snake and her body begged for her to bound from the bed and run for the door. *It will get you.* It was her voice, but there was something strange about the way it popped into her head like a radio getting the sound from a faraway station.

A rustling moved toward her and all she could do was close her eyes tight until the bridge of her nose burned from the effort. The sound stopped—no movements at all. She thought it was gone but before she could believe herself, she heard its breathing close to her ear. Its raspy breaths pushed air in and out like it was on a machine.

Her father's last days behind hospital glass came back in a rush. Although she worked hard to trap the hurt part of herself in a room, that angry, grieving side of her tried to escape its prison.

Her mind saw the machine that breathed for her daddy and remembered its scary wheeze. The image caused her to touch the silver bracelet the way some kids reached for a security blanket.

The bed gave slightly when the thing rested on it and moved closer. She smelled its odor. Whether from its body or its mouth, she couldn't tell, but it was bad. So bad she wanted to cover her nose and mouth. When the smell became too much to stand, it spoke.

"Hungry," a voice closer to a growl whispered. Tabitha clutched her bedspread until fingernails dug into her palms. *Please don't eat me!* Warm air lingered on her cheeks, then whatever spoke, slid off the bed. A door creaked, followed by the snap of a door shutting. Tabitha let out an exhausted breath. She panted in the darkness until the mercy of sleep took hold.

In the morning light, her mother and Eli stood in front of the cellar door with Tabitha further away. She hoped she was safe enough away to escape if the thing ran across the hall after her.

Although the basement door had delicate carvings on the front, the aged finish gave it an old look.

"What are we looking at?" Eli asked without patience.

Tabitha wanted to get her mother aside to talk about the night before, but Eli had his own ideas and stepped between them.

"The door opened while I was in bed," she said, hoping her stepfather wouldn't resort to slapping. *Would he do that in front of her mother?*

"So, the door opened by itself?" Nikki asked.

"What are we listening to? This is stupid," Eli said and raised his arms into the air in disgust.

Nikki threw her husband an irritated expression that Tabitha saw.

"Okay," Eli said, leaned down to the cellar door, and analyzed it like a doctor examining a patient. "Do you see the crack running along the perimeter of the door?" Eli turned from the door to Tabitha. She did her best to see what he saw.

"No."

"Me neither. Because there isn't one."

"I don't understand," Nikki admitted.

Eli ran his finger around the outer edge of the door. "There's no opening. The door and the frame are one solid piece of wood."

"How's that possible? Why does it have a knob and lock if the door won't open?" Nikki asked.

"It was never meant to. The realtor told us this house had a crawl space. This door is for decoration," Eli said and tugged at the handle to show it wouldn't open.

"Then how did it open last night?" Nikki asked.

"I promise you, it opened," Tabitha said.

"Imagination or a dream?" Nikki asked Eli as much as Tabitha.

"It's okay," Nikki said with a smile that didn't vanish until her daughter returned one.

When Tabitha saw the cellar door wasn't a door, she felt stupid. But deep in the night, the worry came back. The memory of the creature's visit—dream or not—had power over her again.

Getting the room across from that door was bad luck. She told herself that the basement thing was imagination. Until the sound of the handle jiggled in the darkness again.

One second she was drifting off, and the next she was wide awake and clamping tight onto her covers.

She heard a snap of a door opening that wasn't supposed to be able to.

"Should I confront the thing? Throw stuffed animals at it until it runs back into the cellar?" she whispered. "I can scream. Then they would see for themselves."

Something occurred to her. What if she screamed and got her mom's attention? She'd come running and the thing would get her. What if it hurt her? Tabitha shook her head to get rid of the idea. She traced the lettering of her bracelet—*Daddy Loves You*—with her finger but pushed him from her mind.

A scraping against the wood floor returned along with whispers except the creature wasn't heading into her room this time.

A rush of relief drenched her, but she listened to where it *was* going.

It was down the hall and took forever in her mind. She heard the front door open. *Go lock the door. Keep it out.* She couldn't get herself to leave the safety of her bed. It won't come back. She lay there, praying that it was gone for good, until sleep finally arrived.

Tabitha wasn't sure she wanted to be awake or asleep. Each scared her. She stepped between the two like a tightrope walker, hoping not to fall.

"Are you going to deal with her or am I?" Eli shouted.

When Tabitha snapped awake, both her mother and stepfather were in front of the cellar door. Their backs to her bedroom. They were talking about her, but she didn't know why they would until she remembered the creature.

Sliding off her bed, she grabbed a stuffed teddy bear. "You'll look after me," she said in a whisper. "Is something wrong?" she asked when she joined the adults in the hallway.

When they turned, she saw between them and lost her breath. Her eyes strayed to the front door and saw a wide trail of mud. The path weaved along the hall and ended at the cellar door.

"Do you think you're funny?" Eli asked and took a step toward the child. "Because I don't think you are."

Nikki put her hand on Eli's chest, but he quickly batted it away.

His movements didn't stop until he was face to face with Tabitha. "You wanna screw with me?" Eli asked and shifted from Tabitha to his wife.

"I didn't…" Tabitha tried to make herself small.

"Maybe something is going on here," Nikki said.

Eli turned to Nikki with his upper set of teeth grinding the lower set. "We can find a way to open this door and—"

"And wreck my house? Break apart a fake door so that this little shit can have a laugh?"

"The house is in my name," Nikki said. Eli slapped her hard enough to send her back against a wall. She pressed a palm to her cheek—tears already welled.

Nikki swiveled from Eli to Tabitha and walked from the hallway. When Tabitha craned her neck to Eli, a smile already formed on his face. But it was his eyes that dared the girl to talk back. She didn't.

They sat around the dinner table together, peering down at the food. Silence was the hardest for the little girl to endure. Tabitha waited patiently for her mother to mention what Eli had done to her. She didn't. It was as if it never happened.

The way Eli acted at dinner told her that was his feeling, too. If her mother was going to pretend Eli never hit her, then she planned to keep quiet about what Eli did to her.

Her mom never looked at her and when the weirdness became too much, Tabitha made up a story about not feeling good just to go to bed early. The excuse was what everybody wanted, and the little girl headed to her bedroom.

There was no story that evening. No tucking in. Not even a kiss goodnight. The adults stayed in their part of the house while she lay alone in the dark, wondering what she did wrong.

Thoughts circled back hundreds of times that night by the time the cellar door creaked and this time she wanted to know what was inside that door. What brought it there? And where did it go? She couldn't unravel the story.

She held her breath and waited to see the direction the crawling sound would take. To her relief, it was to the front door again. When the front door opened, and she was half-sure the hallway was clear, Tabitha pushed her covers aside and touched the cold floor with the tips of her toes.

When she thought of the cellar door, a single idea came to her. As she crept closer to the hall, the thought was too logical to dismiss. If the door was solid during the day, wouldn't it stay open at night when the *thing* was outside?

She gazed at the front door—wide open to the night—with no creature around. Tabitha's stomach churned when she headed to the door that was a door again. A crack led all the way around. Laying a hand on the knob, she remembered how someone stopped her from turning it.

Was there more than one creature? Would it be waiting inside for her? She felt stupid for not thinking there could be more, but it was too late. She had to know.

The handle turned easy. No one tried to stop her as the latch clicked like it was a new mechanism instead of an antique. The wooden façade glided open.

A small patch of light revealed a staircase going down, turning left, and going down further. Seeing the stairs going so deep told her that wherever this place was, it didn't belong to the house. Someone may have added the basement and stairs, but it felt like it belonged to a fairy tale.

She turned her father's silver bracelet around her wrist several times. *Don't think about him.* She stepped down the narrow staircase. Although the wood was old, it never gave under her weight. Down she went, as the flight spiraled left many times until she settled onto a dirt floor. Shuffling her feet, she kicked up dirt.

There wasn't light, but she found she could see. Her head shifted to make sense of how her eyes worked so deep underground.

The ground below felt funny under her. Hunched down on folded legs, she pushed the dirt aside and found a hard floor. She knocked on it and heard the dull sound of wood.

When she rose, a door stood closed in front of her. The door and walls didn't belong. They shouldn't have been there.

Before she could complete one step toward the door, a sound at the top of the staircase brought her back to reality. The thing was coming for her, and she had nowhere to go.

The sound grew louder, and all she could do was push herself against the wall and remain still. If she stayed still it might not see her. It was a fragile plan, but all she had.

The creature dropped from the landing, and something made a thud after. It passed in front of her, breathing hard as it dragged something behind.

In her nervousness, Tabitha flicked her silver bracelet, and it made a jingling sound. The creature stopped in its tracks, gazed around, and sniffed the air. Tabitha didn't move—didn't breathe—and prayed the thing would keep moving.

Instead, it turned back and bent down on deformed legs. The thing tore into the flesh of an opossum it had dragged into the house and down the stairs.

On the head of the creature was a long mane of hair. The face she couldn't see, but the sound of tearing flesh told her all she needed. If she weren't careful, she'd be next. Its eating continued with teeth sinking into flesh. Bone snapped under the weight of its jaw.

Leaning against the icy wall, and breathing in the copper smell of the animal's blood, made her woozy. Her legs were young, but the wobble told her she wouldn't be standing on them much longer.

Her knees dipped. When she accepted her fate, the thing dragged the animal toward the door. It opened it, and the creature took its treasure inside a room, slamming the door as it went.

Tabitha fell to the dirt floor. She panted fast, but kept as quiet as she could. She came close to bad things, and wanted nothing more to do with the creature. A fog blanketed her mind with every step that led her back to the safety of her bedroom.

The next morning was a fog she drifted through. Every meal, or moment of quiet she pretended to be okay but felt dead inside. But no matter how hard she tried to push the creature from her thoughts, she failed. Something so dark and hungry, living right under her feet, was more than she could stand.

Things like that don't exist. She tried to convince herself and couldn't. The creature had always been under the nose of humans. People weren't open to the possibility.

Her mom and Eli wouldn't believe her, and meeting the thing in the cellar again would be the end. What choice did she have? When hunger became too much to bear for the basement dweller, Tabitha would find herself on its menu.

Each night in the new house added more terror to Tabitha. The fear of the unknown slithered her past into view. The more she refused to think about the dad she lost, the more power the basement thing got.

They were growing together even if she didn't know how. She lay in bed thinking of the teeth sinking into the poor opossum's body, along with the snapping of its bone and ligaments. The memory stirred her anxiety.

A crying woman roused her from the dark thoughts. Sitting straight up in her bed, Tabitha listened for any hint to where the pathetic sobs came from. When the moans got louder, she was never going to remain in the bed.

As she made it into the hallway, the woman's voice confused her.

It wasn't coming from the cellar door as she thought.

Following the high-pitched cries, she walked deeper into her home until she stopped in front of her parent's room. Swinging the door open with all her might, Tabitha found Eli on top of her mother.

It was like walking into a scary movie. Eli slammed his fist into her mother's face, with blood immediately gushing. Tabitha tried to understand but made no sense of what she saw.

"Mom?"

Her mother lifted her head toward the small voice, as if attached to wires. She tried to speak but failed as another blow from her husband landed on her jaw.

"Go," was all her mother could get out.

There was nothing Tabitha could do to stop Eli, but she ran at him anyway. A thought popped into her head—weak and meaningless. She grabbed his hair with both hands and yanked with all the strength of a little girl. The smell of beer was strong on his breath.

His head went back hard, and her power surprised her. The tug didn't quite pull her stepfather off, but it got his attention.

A step back was her one defense. When Eli lowered his head and got to his feet. Her mother screamed behind him.

"Leave her alone!"

If Eli heard her pleas, he never showed it in his grim expression. He grabbed the child by the shoulder and swung his arm. Whipping air came first then a palm to the side of Tabitha's face.

"You're an interfering little bitch," Eli said and prepared to punish her again when her mother stepped between them.

"Don't touch my daughter," she shouted and tore Tabitha loose.

Eli stood, staring at a broken silver bracelet that came away in his hand. He flung the jewelry into the hallway as his wife shoved her daughter out the door. Panic caught hold of Tabitha when she realized her mom was closing herself inside. She'd never seen her mother so afraid.

"I'll be fine. Go to bed now," she commanded.

Tabitha stared at the door as the sound of slaps returned from the other side.

Tabitha sat with a flashlight on her lap, working on her bracelet. She didn't know how long her mother's screams lasted, but it felt like it went on forever. When the image of Eli hitting her mom returned, she swept it away. She thought of the sweetness of her stuffed animals, the gentle way her father would wrap her into his chest. Anything to keep her mother far from her mind.

A paperclip was the best way for her to fix the silver chain. She was happy with her handy work and read the words, *Daddy Loves You*. She placed her face in her hands and cried. She wished he were there to help her now. Although it was late into the night, she would never sleep.

All her fears vanished when the cellar door jiggled. For the first time since the creature's arrival, relief swallowed her whole. The creature was more than a frightening monster. Her unhappiness with Eli gave it power. When she saw her stepfather hit her mother, she felt a connection with the creature she couldn't explain.

As the creature made its familiar appearance and headed for the door to hunt for food, her child's toes hit the floor. She made it swiftly to the basement door as fast as her legs would carry her. She swung the door wide, let the knob hit the wall, and propelled herself forward. She planted her feet wide the way a baseball catcher might when expecting a fastball. Drawing air into her lungs, she let it all out in a roar.

"Eli!" she screamed. "Asshole…Eli!" She let every syllable have it. Tabitha repeated her shriek twice more before she heard the footsteps of a man heading her way. Swiveling on the balls of her feet, she took a step down the dark staircase.

When Eli saw the door standing wide open, his jaw dropped.

"What the fuck is going on?" he whispered to himself.

Clenching his fist and biting his lip, Eli rushed through the doorway that was never there the day before.

Tabitha heard her stepfather above her on the stairs coming down. She needed to move quickly but she couldn't get her feet to work in the dark. He was getting closer. She pumped her legs but didn't expect the last stair to disappear. She awkwardly stepped onto the floor of the basement. Finding solid ground so fast caused her body to sprawl forward, splashing onto the dirt floor.

Above her, Eli took the steps two and three at a time. Knees already echoed their pain as she scrambled to her feet, pushing through the mysterious door, and slamming it closed behind her.

Tabitha searched for a lock to keep Eli out but found nothing. She spun on her heels to find something that could save her, and what she saw chilled her blood.

Circling the basement room, on every shelf sat stuffed animals like the ones she owned. These plush toys had aged badly— shades of black and green covered the material. Rotting from the moisture of the basement and giving the bears, a dolphin, and other animals a slimy texture.

"Wait," she spoke to herself and forgot her pursuer. "This is my room."

Her mouth opened when she saw the bedspread—filthy from neglect but the same pattern as the one upstairs. Situated around the room were dolls she owned. Posters she'd picked out lined the walls. Returning her gaze to the door, she was sure she was inside her bedroom. Her bedroom but somehow from long ago.

The first loud footsteps broke her away from her astonishment and the mirror image of her room. Ideas ran through her mind. Hide behind the door. Slip under the bed. Cover herself with a blanket.

Before she could settle on a plan, Eli opened the door. He stood in the doorway panting from his run but more likely breathing heavily from anger.

"Leave me alone, Eli," she said, and pointed in the angriest gesture she could.

"You call me Dad." He showed his teeth, but there was no humor in his expression.

"You're not my dad. Mine was special. You're just a stranger!" Whatever response she expected from him, it didn't match his reaction. Eli flashed deep sadness and let his face turn back to a vicious scowl.

"No matter." A happy façade returned to his face. "I'll teach you." He took a step into the room and toward Tabitha.

Crossing her arms defensively and stepping back, she had already resigned herself to whatever was in store for her. Eli ran for the child, zeroing in on her face. When his hand clutched her, his eyes opened wide.

Teeth sunk into the top of his shoulder. It was the creature. Her stepfather squirmed wildly in the bedroom to remove the hungry mouth from his meaty flesh. When he yanked himself free, a huge chunk of skin came away on the thing's lips.

Eli fell to the floor and held tight to the wound with blood pouring onto the dirt floor. His frightened expression was far away. The creature stood in front of Eli and continued to chew on his skin.

"Thank you. You're my protector. Aren't you?" Tabitha asked.

For a moment, the creature stopped chewing and turned its head her way. The little girl walked closer to her rescuer and listened to its breathing. The sudden movement jolted the creature's frame. With warped legs, the thing rushed through the wooden replica of her door.

"Wait. Who are you?" Tabitha could see teeth through greasy black hair and nothing more.

"Eat," the thing said in a growl and pointed toward Eli's dying body. The basement thing slowly shut the door. As the creature disappeared, Tabitha glimpsed something shimmery on its wrist. A tarnished silver bracelet with a paperclip holding it together. She saw the etched words: *Daddy Loves You.*

As the door shut tight, she gazed down at her bracelet fastened around her wrist and began to understand. She'd imprisoned her grieving part—safe from the light. Until then. She never understood the threat until she tried to open the door. It was no use. This was her new home.

~ THE IDIOT BOX ~

A car crash threatened Jeff Solomon's life. But as luck would have it, he hobbled away with only a broken leg. He had a new lease on life, but the boredom inside a house was too much to take.

The average citizen slid into a chair, grabbed a remote control, and sunk into oblivion. But Jeff was different. He refused to watch it. This decision mystified others, but no one as much as his best friend, Charlie. His friend thought television was a window to view modern life. In the twenty-first century, televisions were as common as a toilet. Although Jeff didn't believe owning a boob tube was the same as worshipping a golden calf, he still found he had little use for the thing.

"You're just not whole without experiencing a television," Charlie would say with some humor and a streak of seriousness that Jeff always detected underneath. "You'll never be able to read people as I can," Charlie said.

Jeff laughed Charlie's comments off. Charlie flipped burgers at the local diner. An honest profession, but he was sure Charlie didn't have the smarts for much more of a challenge than cooking.

Jeff sat in front of his first television. Not because of the constant pressure from people like Charlie or because of the shear boredom his injury caused him. He was simply curious of what all the fuss was about.

At dinner parties, parents would always admit their child was obsessed with devices. Jeff was so behind the curve he didn't even think kids watched television anymore. Phones and tablets were in every child's hand. They were a plague.

Jeff wanted to join the mainstream world, but thought of himself as the reverse of progress. He ordered a pizza and lined up a six-pack of Bud Light—in a bottle. He loved them in a bottle. The cans just tasted funny to him, like he could taste the metal from the aluminum. He didn't think it possible, but he bought the bottles just in case.

He placed the pizza box in front of him and lifted the cardboard lid to reveal the cheesy delight within. He'd planned this event with all the foresight of a general preparing for conquest. Jeff's mind thought about the cable guy's question.

"You want me to set the channels on the television for you? It's not a problem," he'd said.

Jeff's mind couldn't react to the inquiry. *Don't they have all the channels built into the set?* he wanted to ask the installer. He suspected the cable guy would regard him as a Martian new to Earth. Instead, he gave a subtle nod that sent the cable guy into a barrage of movements and gestures.

His involvement with the remote control caused the channels to blink from one to the next, snow-filled to clear—so quickly a person prone to epilepsy would have fallen into a coma.

When the installer finished, he killed the picture and handed off the remote to Jeff like the Spear of Destiny.

Jeff thanked the cable magician and prayed he didn't come off like a caveman frightened by fire. He felt he came out unscathed by the exchange, but who could know?

He hoisted a slice of pizza to his mouth and watched the tip of the pie slump below his lips. It pointed toward the floor. He arched his wrist above his head and slid the glistening wonder between his gaping teeth. His eyes rolled back into his head as the warm delicacy melted onto his tongue. He smelled the food and relished every moment. *Nothing like a pizza.* Jeff put down the slice, popped open the cap on the beer bottle, and took a swig, feeling the angry carbonation tickle his tongue before it drained to his stomach. Without forcing himself, a belch erupted from him without notice.

He eyed the remote control beside the future beers he would soon drink. He nodded his head as if answering the controller itself. "Alright." He picked up the remote and found the orange power button with his thumb, pressing the rubber circle down. The television came to life in a neon glow. Jeff squinted in the dim room.

His eyes adjusted to the screen when a woman appeared and stretched downward, pressing her chest into her knees. The woman revealed her backside to the audience like her ass was doing the talking. Jeff couldn't believe his eyes.

Women and men did the same thing in a circle around her. Not that Jeff never saw people in an aerobics class or that he never saw a dirty magazine—he'd seen both. Something else got to him. The extreme close-ups messed with him. The way the camera would zoom into the women's tight breasts or the curves that led to her inner thigh. It was like the cameraman manipulated where his eyes focused. His pulse went up like connected to live wires.

He tried not to remain on the girl's body but inevitably he reverted to the taboo places. To Jeff, it was learning your instincts all over again. From the age of a teenager, he learned that staring at a woman's cleavage wasn't appropriate. Here he was, a student once more, learning right from wrong.

Jeff searched the remote for a button that would switch the channel and placed a digit on it. The channel moved to the next in the number order. On the screen, he saw a family ordering a pizza from the same place he did an hour before. The commercial showed the toppings, and then, for one inexplicable moment, the camera leaned in for a better angle at the mother's ample chest.

"What the hell?" he asked. His eyes didn't leave her cleavage until the scene changed to another commercial. As the next ad continued, his eyes scanned for the female.

"This isn't me."

He was a voyeur, and he understood what the thrill of television was. To watch someone when they didn't know you were watching. His father's voice tumbled into his head. *This sinful contraption will pull your soul down into the bowels of hell!*

For the first time since adulthood, Jeff agreed with all his heart. Guilt rushed through Jeff as one scantily dressed woman after another sashayed to the side of the screen.

Panic filled him from an alien place. He pushed the power button and heard the television make a whooshing sound before it went black. For a moment, it crackled with static electricity, and he watched himself in the black mirror of the television. He thought the sound resembled the same noise the candy *Pop Rocks* would make when a child would empty a whole packet into their mouth. He carried the thirty-five-inch LG into the spare bedroom and propped it onto an old file cabinet.

The electric cord wrapped around the set like a snake constricting its victim. The end of the cord stared at Jeff with its deadly three-pronged face.

That was the last time he watched the television, and he was glad for it. He'd still feel a pang of regret when the cable bill came every month. His service agreement was due to continue for another year. But that was okay to him—lesson learned.

Charlie walked through the door as he had for the last ten years. It was a friendly moment they shared before they started their days. Charlie would eat his breakfast with Jeff and walk to the diner to start his workday, and Jeff to his job at the pharmacy.

Of course, since he'd been on sick leave, he had gone nowhere but to the couch. Still, Jeff was happy that their little routine survived the accident. Their mornings together made him feel safe somehow. Jeff's ex-girlfriend Sharon never understood this ritual of theirs. And what she didn't understand compelled her to destroy it.

"I'm with you now," she would say. "We don't need no grown man coming into our house to have breakfast with you every morning. It looks funny like you are a…you know," Sharon said, and not trying to be subtle.

It never worked out with Sharon. Not because she disliked Charlie, but that didn't help matters. Jeff thought she was a bad person who constantly complained they didn't have the latest widescreen beauty on the wall.

She concealed her faults, like a magician pulling the wool over the eyes of the audience but he saw through her. Her conversations gave her away to Jeff.   She was a dam that seeped continuous water forever without allowing the entire payload to break through. He remembered snippets of bile that made its way past the breach.

Sharon's feelings on orphans, vagabonds, fast food workers, and people on welfare were disturbing. Her entire attitude made Jeff sick to his stomach and became an emotional border.

Although he gave Sharon the old heave-ho, she came around every once in a while to worm her way back in. No one had ever turned Sharon away in her life. If she were the one who did the dumping, he never would have seen her again.

"I'm starving, Jeffy boy," Charlie said, making the toast while Jeff manned the eggs.

"Me too," Jeff agreed while he scanned the newspaper folded in half. A headline caught his attention, and he read. The crackle of the eggs slowed his train of thought. He scooped up the hard eggs with a spatula and tossed them onto a plate.

"Listen to this, Charlie." Jeff read, "Astrologers discovered a solar flare from a dying sun a million light-years away. The large star engulfed its solar system before its cataclysmic event and traveled through the universe."

Charlie wiped butter across the four pieces of toast.

"You're not putting too much butter on mine, are you, Charlie?"

"Nope, not at all," he said as a part of their normal routine.

"Do you understand what this means?"

Charlie shook his head.

"Before we were born, before any man was born, this event happened, and just now, the light is reaching Earth. Isn't that amazing?"

"Yeah, amazing, Jeffy." Charlie scooped the eggs and piled them onto toast.

"Alright, fine." Jeff gave up his attempt to enlighten and couldn't believe the speed Charlie pushed food down his throat. "Easy tiger. Nobody's going to take that from you," he teased.

"Bill might," Charlie said between forked bites of eggs.

"What's that, Charlie?"

"Bill the mailman; he might. On my way here, I saw him with an enormous piece of meat."

"So?" he asked as he squished his toast against a hill of eggs as leverage for his fork.

"Bill was burying it in his yard."

Jeff's ears perked up. "You had to be mistaken."

Charlie's head twisted back and forth, and he glimpsed the bags under the eyes. It was his skin that caught Jeff's attention. It was darker somehow, like a fine film. He let the ridiculous idea go.

"Bill was on all fours, like a dog digging in his backyard. He held onto the long meat like I was going to take it. I tried to turn away, but I couldn't. Bill had an angry face as he dug with his hands. He put the meat into the ground and covered it back up. He growled at me too before he ran into his house."

He didn't know what to do with Charlie's information. "That *is* strange," he admitted. "I kind of don't believe it."

Charlie slid the last of his breakfast into his mouth and washed it down with some *Sunny Delight*. "Well, it's the truth. I gotta go, Jeffy. My boss said if I'm late one more time, he'll tan my hide, whatever that means."

"Then, you better go."

Charlie headed for the door. "When is your cast coming off?" he called back.

"The doc says it happens next week. You want to hang tonight?" he asked.

"Sorry, tonight's a *Brady Bunch* marathon."

Jeff smiled at the confession. "Right. See you tomorrow, Charlie."

With Charlie gone, he didn't know what to do with the ocean of time in front of him. He shuffled through magazines and attempted to read the latest copy of a Stephen King novel for the second time. After he knew an ending, the thrill of the chase— gone. The thought of Bill's odd behavior returned to his mind. *What was he doing?* Jeff peered at his wall of periodicals with contempt.

"I need out of here." Jeff hobbled over to a drawer next to the kitchen sink. He yanked out a few tools and prepared for the removal of his plaster prison. The leg was free an hour later. He studied his shriveled leg that resembled the pale white of a corpse.

"Gross!"

He tested the stability of the leg with his weight. It held, but he needed his antique cane—bought at a yard sale years before.

Jeff liked the Saint Bernard carved into the wood top and he would never have guessed he would have to use it to walk. Several times he tried to lean on the cane for support before he understood where he needed to focus his weight. He managed and headed for the door for the first time in weeks.

The neighborhood had an ominous quiet for a summer morning. He expected neighbors to be working on their lawns, or children playing outside at the very least. Nothing, no movement. He walked slowly past the line of houses and headed down a back alley that led to Bill's house. He watched Bill's home grow larger with each delicate step that brought him closer.

In front of the chain-link fence, he studied the mound of brown dirt in the center of the green grass. He shifted his eyes from the mound and back to Bill's home.

"Here we go," he said, without an optimistic tone. Jeff leaned forward over the fence and used gravity to help his cause. The top half of his body propelled past the top rail with his weight dragging the bottom half over.

He hit the manicured lawn hard enough to take the wind from him. The fall jolted his leg, enough to wonder if it had caused any further damage.

When the pain subsided, relief took its place. Suffering through another stretch in a cast was more than he could stand. Back on his feet, he staggered to the mound and stole one last glance at Bill's home.

He dug into the dirt with his hands, feeling the cold earth between his fingers. Glancing up once or twice while he pushed dirt from the hole. When his hands touched the meat, the clammy flesh startled him to a stop. Continuing to dig, he pulled the meat from its shallow grave, wiped the dirt off, and stared at the huge bone. He understood for the first time what he held in his hands and threw it in front of him before pushing himself back.

Staring at the human leg, a woman's leg, melted his resolve. He couldn't be sure who it belonged to, but logic told him it was the mailman's wife.

Pulling himself up with help from the cane, he backed away from the leg and wanted nothing more to do with whatever happened there. The house took on an evil expression when it gazed back at him.

He imagined Bill running from the doorway toward him with arms flailing and a butcher's knife. This image motivated Jeff to pull his full weight onto his leg and clear the fence with no problem this go-round.

At the police station, Jeff's brother stared back at him with seriousness.

"Did you get the leg?" Carl asked. The question infuriated him, but it was also a question he would have asked.

"No, I didn't," he admitted. "But when we go back there…"

"Whoa, whoa. You are on sick leave, and you are not involved and not an officer," Carl said.

"Who gives two shits what I am. You have a gun—therefore *I* have one. I can swing by my place and get mine," Jeff said.

Carl peered at the face of his hobbled brother and smiled. "I'll tell you what…I'll check it out and call you the moment I find out anything."

Jeff shook his head.

"I'll keep you in the loop. It's the best I can do without losing my job and pension."

Jeff realized his brother's dilemma and accepted. "Alright. But you better call the very second you find something. Or it will be your death."

"No sweat." Carl nodded.

When Jeff looked around the precinct it stunned him. The place was like a ghost town. Most desks were empty.

"Where's everyone?" he asked.

Carl gave Jeff an uneasy expression. "It's the freakiest thing. Most of the force called in sick, and half of those never called in at all."

"No call, no show?" Jeff asked.

"I know. I can't remember the last time an officer never bothered to call in sick. The flu's going around, maybe?" Carl said, but Jeff heard doubt in his voice. "Get home and off your feet. I'll call. Don't worry. Your brother's on it."

Jeff scrunched up his face.

"I feel better already."

When Jeff woke from his nap, the day was gone. A red icon appeared on his phone and with a quick gesture, a familiar voice sprung to life in his living room.

"Jeff! I went to the mailman's house, and he wasn't home. I found the hole in the backyard, but no leg. That doesn't mean it wasn't there. But I have a more pressing problem. The switchboard lit up after you left with calls of attacks from everywhere. Do me a favor and stay in your house and lock your doors. Don't leave, no matter what. And don't worry, I'll go check on Charlie for you." The voicemail ended.

"Charlie!" He dialed the phone and listened as the line rang on. "Come on Charlie." His friend never answered.

From outside came a faint noise like a muffled scream. He concentrated on the sound and blocked everything else out.

A loud knock on the door shook his nerves with the jolt. Fumbling for the door, he slid his eye onto the peephole. Although he couldn't make out the features, he was sure a woman was on his porch.

"Who's there?" he asked. The figure remained silent. The woman never answered and never budged. She stood there in the gloom swaying.

"Are you in trouble? Do you need help?" The female continued to sway. "I'm opening the door, but I want you to stay back so we can talk. Okay?"

He placed a finger on the deadbolt and twisted. It turned easily in his grip. When he pulled the door from its frame, the porch was empty in the moonlight.

He released air with a heavy sigh and swung the door. Before the door met the frame, a heavy thud rocked the other side and swung it back his direction. The impact tossed Jeff to the carpet below.

"Sharon?" he asked, not sure of himself. His ex-girlfriend lumbered into the living room, past him as if she didn't notice him on the floor at all. Her expression was ferocious, the way an animal might curl its lips up when confronted with an enemy.

Brown lumps grew along her neck, jawbone, and forehead. He moved back toward the wall and gave himself some distance. "What happened to you?"

She staggered closer, seeing him for the first time. She studied him as if gazing into a mirror.

Hair jutted in every direction from her skin. He would have sworn he could see hair spreading over her. It was the appearance of an ape, but not the kind at a zoo. An image from the movie *Planet of the Apes* entered his brain. She was an ape with human features. He didn't want her there any longer.

"Food." She spoke as if there was something lodged in her throat.

"Sure, I'll get you something to eat," he said and hurried to the kitchen. Sharon followed him with ambling movements that made his heart race. "No, that's okay, I can get it myself. Just stay where you are," he pleaded. But she didn't stay. "Stop moving."

In a panic, he bolted for the kitchen and searched for anything useful. Before he found a weapon, Sharon threw her arms around his waist with teeth sinking into his thigh. She tore away a swatch of his jeans and pinched his skin in the process.

Jeff swiveled his head back and forth for something to grab and spotted a rolling pin. He pushed himself forward and grabbed the handle just as she returned her gaping mouth to his thigh. This time, her teeth sunk deep into the skin. The pain almost caused him to loosen his grip on the pin.

He slammed the wooden roller against her skull with as much strength as he could. Her teeth no longer clamped onto him, as a dull expression captured her face. When she fell to the floor it was like a stuffed animal.

The damage on his thigh was minor—slight bleeding at most. He stood there watching his ex-girlfriend twitching below him and couldn't turn away.

He needed to know what was happening outside and his phone didn't even have internet. *The Radio.* Snapping on the dial, he guided the radio knob past the crackle as if the station were taking a breath. On a local station, a group of speakers squawked loud and interrupted each other.

Jeff listened to the commentators bicker and all the while searching for a rope to tie Sharon's hands. If she woke up, he wasn't sure what he'd have to do to her. It took some time, but he found enough twine to do the job. He twisted it around her several times before he felt safe.

He studied his handiwork, then tied her hands for good measure. He leaned against the kitchen sink and listened closer to the commentator's conversation.

"I think this rash of cannibalistic murders in our town is a viral infection like the outbreak of the AIDS," a voice shouted over the airways a moment before another voice interrupted.

"Ridiculous! This outbreak has nothing to do with the natural world."

"Then what caused it?" a third voice demanded.

"I think it's the star that exploded in another galaxy." Laughter erupted all around from the group. "Think about it, the moment the light from that star reached Earth, the chaos started." More laughter soared above the comment.

"I know we have to be daring with our ideas, but that's just stupid," a voice said.

Jeff cut off the radio and stared at the woman he once loved. Fur completely covered her face and neck. He scooted a chair close and aligned his eyes to hers.

"What happened to you?" When she glanced up, he was positive she was really seeing him. "Answer me."

"I was watching television," she said, as if the words were foreign or she had discovered the language for the first time. "Felt a shock in me from the screen. I got so hungry." She stopped and recognized Jeff. Saliva fell from her open mouth. "You're my food," she said.

He moved away from Sharon. Momentarily forgetting that she was bound. He remembered the television set in his spare bedroom. When he brought it into his arms dust flew in every direction as he unwrapped the cord, plugged the end into the receptacle, and secured the cable line. He sat motionless in front of the television but couldn't bring himself to turn the thing on. His father's voice returned. *I won't bring evil into this house.*

"You were right, Pop," Jeff said and aimed the screen toward Sharon. Facing away from the display and into her eyes, he pressed the power button.

The television came to life. Sharon's face shone with an eerie glow. At first, she avoided the screen, but soon she focused all her attention on the program. She wasn't exactly watching the television anymore, but she drew something else from it.

Black hairs sprouted from her pores in places he would have sworn before that day hair couldn't grow—shouldn't grow. He had the urge to pull the cord from the wall and end the freak show, but he had to see what the television would do to her.

All at once, his body tingled either from the crazy show or a contagion. He rubbed his arms, then the back of his neck, and felt no hair growing. A sigh of relief escaped him.

Sharon's hair grew. Her arms elongated inches more than normal. To Jeff, it resembled someone who inflated a basketball with too much air.

Her back contorted in an unnatural position until her spine protruded like the sharp edges of a spear.

"Sharon? Can you hear me?" Jeff asked. Guilt wrapped around him and threatened to suffocate.

Her eyes bulged from the sockets like they were not meant for her body anymore. Her tongue stretched from her mouth and took the shape of a serpent. The tongue forked supernaturally, splitting apart as he watched with bewilderment.

He'd seen enough. In a moment of anger, he kicked the television until it slid hard off the table and crashed to the tile floor below. The plastic shell collapsed, sparks rose, and the thing was a broken heap. Whatever reaction the television started continued in Sharon's body.

"Maybe the crackpots on the radio were right. Was it the light from a dying solar system?" She said nothing. An image of a force stronger than a billion nuclear missiles propelling souls through the universe appeared in Jeff's mind. "Yesterday, the first light of that long-dead world visited Earth. Then, somehow they made their way through the televisions to a waiting host? Sounds like something from *Creepshow* or *Tales from the Crypt*," he said and laughed.

Jeff limped into his bedroom, opened his sock drawer, and stared at his revolver. He plucked the gun from its hiding place and felt the cold steel in his hands.

Before the urge that led him to the gun vanished, he stood in front of the Sharon that was no longer like herself, or any human he'd ever known.

Her bulging eyes stared at Jeff as he pointed the pistol. Placing a finger on the trigger, she moved her mouth to speak. The words came out in harsh grunts except for one.

"Jeff," she said.

Closing his eyes over his tears, he pulled the trigger and watched Sharon slump onto the floor.

"One more stop tonight," he said.

Charlie's home was normal except for Carl's police car parked by the curb. Not a good sign considering he tried to call his brother all night and got no answer.

He walked up the path leading to Charlie's ranch-style house and wondered how many people had turned on their television that night in search of answers? How many children, taken in by the glow of their cell phones?

The lights were on in Charlie's place. Did he see movement? As he continued up the stone path to the door, he found it half-open.

"Shit."

Squeezing through the doorway and pulling out his revolver, he walked on shaky legs into the living room. A television blared across the room, facing him like a rabid dog. Jeff shielded his face from the set and kept his eyes away from the night's program.

How long before a human started feeling the effects of the television broadcast? He didn't want to know.

Like slushing through mud, he entered the living room as if he were wearing concrete shoes. Holding a gun inside his best friend's place was unnatural and he never thought about what he'd do if he found him.

A sight stopped him cold. His brother's police hat sat on a chair. With trembling hands, Jeff lifted it for a closer look. Dried blood covered the top and hinted at a story he was afraid to learn.

"Carl?" Tears filled his eyes. The house remained quiet except for the television behind him. "Carl? Charlie?"

He didn't want to move anymore and thought about leaving altogether until a noise broke his paralysis. A shuffling of feet on the floor.

Charlie appeared in the doorway that led from the kitchen, walking slowly as he dragged something behind him.

In horror, he understood everything. His best friend, Charlie, had his brother by the arm. Holding Carl's chewed torso, he dragged him closer.

Dull eyes stared back at him as Carl's corpse scraped across the floor. Vomit was already in Jeff's mouth—burning like lava.

Charlie's face was the same. All his contours and features hadn't made the full transformation yet. But it was the blood covering his friend that told another gruesome story.

"I guess that *Brady Bunch* marathon was your downfall," he said with no humor. A tear fell from his eyes as Jeff lifted his gun to Charlie. "I'm so sorry this happened to you." He wiped away the burning tears so he could refocus when a gun rang out.

Jeff went down hard as a bullet tore threw him. He fell to the living room floor without firing a shot.

Confusion mingled with a sting in his stomach and chest. He checked to confirm his worst fear and as he glanced back, smoke billowed from his brother's gun—now in Charlie's hand.

With each step closer, he saw the fur covering Charlie's face. "Stay back, Charlie. I don't want to hurt you," was all he could think of to say. Looking down, Jeff saw his wrecked chest and his gun a foot from his hand. With all his strength, he tried to reach for it. A frightening revelation hit him as hard as the bullet from the gun. *I'm alive but I can't move my body.* The bullet that entered his chest had gone straight through and had damaged his spine. He sat motionless as Charlie leaned inches from his face.

"Guess we won't be having breakfast," Jeff said.

"I will, Jeffy," Charlie said in a raspy voice.

"You always put too much butter on my toast anyway." Charlie's bulged eyes grew wider as he dove onto Jeff's chest and took large bites out of his friend.

"Enjoy the meal." A tear rolled down Jeff's face as Charlie continued to eat.

~THE TEDDY BEAR~

Detective Scott Sedge and Dale Evans watched me during my psychic reading with fascination.

"Sometimes our need to keep someone with us is so strong that no distance is too great to reach. The connection to our loved ones has an elasticity. Wherever they are or whatever they're doing, we can move beyond time and space to pull them to us.

"I'm going to focus my thoughts on the things around me. The atmosphere—the essence of the natural world." I stood there wavering in place a long time.

The detectives gave each other a knowing glance.

"I will leave him to you then," Sedge said and handed me off to Dale like a child lost in a grocery store.

"Whatcha see there, boss?" Dale said in an accent that wasn't quite Southern.

"Is that where the child was last seen?" I pointed to a picnic table. SWAM

Detective Dale Evans nodded.

I placed my hand where they said the child sat.

"The origin of the vanishing holds the strongest energy," I whispered, and held my head skyward. "I'm channeling the tether now."

"Tether? We're trying to find a little boy," Dale said.

"As am I, Detective." The other officers, mostly in blue uniforms, gathered around the crime scene and pointed. I heard their snickers. Every time was the same, and I got no credit until they saw with their own eyes what I could do.

"I saw you on the television. You know that?"

"I do now," I said, trying to talk to Dale as little as possible. "I'm afraid there's interference."

"Like an antenna?" Dale said and turned away from me toward the other cops. They laughed at whatever he did with his face.

"Something's blocking my connection to the boy," I corrected. Dale shrugged.

"What do you need from me?" he asked.

"I need to speak to the parents."

The detective rolled his eyes, already shaking me off.

"Listen. I saw them here and I need their positive energy." Dale moved in front of me. His large frame blocked out the street. As I stood there in his shadow, my stomach felt queasy.

"Listen to me, you piece of shit." He looked around and brought his voice down. "My captain said he wanted me to involve you, but I'm not letting you anywhere near grieving parents. Do you hear me?"

"Loud and clear, Dale," I said, sliding a phone from my pocket. I smiled at him as I dialed.

"Who are you calling?"

I ignored him and placed the phone to my ear. When the voicemail recording began, I listened but tried to stay in the performance.

"Voicemail," I added and put it back to the side of my head. "Captain Stewart, this is psychic, Bryar Wilson." I watched Dale fight to get it together. It made me feel warm inside. "The reason I'm—"

"Okay. You'll get your wish," Dale said and threw his hands in the air. "Just hang up."

A smile came back onto my face, but this time it was real. I enjoyed my authority.

"I'll get them…just…"

"I'll be right here."

Detective Evans walked into a crowd of officers and returned with a couple that seemed too young to have a kid.

I extended a hand to the man. It's always the best strategy. If you touch a woman first, the husband will never trust you after that, almost impossible to win back. "I'm Bryar." I nodded my head to Dale as if to say, *do your job*.

"This is Tonya and Craig. Toby's parents."

Get your head in the game, Dale.

"Are you aware of what I do?" I turned to the husband first, then to Tonya.

"No." Craig paced around his wife. "I told these cops that they are wasting time. Toby isn't here anymore. We should be searching somewhere else."

"That's where I come in. I'm a psychic rescuer."

Tonya heard this and raised her head toward me. "So, you can help us find Toby?"

"I've helped hundreds of lost children make it back home."

I ignored Dale's irritated expression.

"We're not sure what he can do yet," Dale said to undercut me.

It didn't matter. I had the couple's full attention.

"Do you have something of Toby's I can touch? It can be anything."

Tonya held out a teddy bear from under her arm and I pretended that I was afraid to touch it with my bare hands. For dramatic effect, I slowly slid my glove off my hand and took the stuffed animal. I felt its soft fur, caressing every part of the material before handing it back to her. Lowering my head and closing my eyes, I absorbed the surrounding sounds. "Baseball. That's what's trying to come into my circle."

"Toby loves baseball," Craig chimed in.

I peeked through the slits of my eyes and saw the Atlanta Braves mascot embroidered on his Jersey. "I'm sensing a baseball team. This is strange. I don't know anything about sports, but I'm seeing Native Americans and baseball. Does that mean anything to you?"

"Yes. He always watched the Atlanta Braves with his dad," Tonya added with me nodding back.

"Does he have a medical issue? The reason I ask is in this bear's shape, I'm feeling tightness in my chest." The chest makes up most of a human body and if there is ever a health problem, I'm covered.

"He was just diagnosed with asthma last year!" Tonya shouted. "Is he okay? Can you see him?"

When I let my eyelids relax, I saw Dale's surprised expression. *Gotcha Dale.*

"I can't yet picture the boy in my mind but…he is alive," I assured them. When I opened my eyes, the young couple held each other. Tears fell to their cheeks.

"I promise you. When I know something more, you will too," I said, grabbed both their hands and squeezed tight. Dale gave me a nod as officers escorted the couple away.

"I can't say I fully believe you, Bryar, but I'm willing to give you the benefit of the doubt."

"That's all Toby and I ask for."

When I got back to my apartment—the top floor, of course— I saw the maid had come and gone. Nothing made me happier than avoiding interactions with the help.

I didn't think I was above them, I just didn't want to deal with the small talk. The everyday lives of strangers made my skin crawl.

As I poured a drink an ache started in my head. I tried to ignore the dull thud and slid into my leather armchair. My first thought was I'd caught a cold—sure, the symptoms came on fast, but what else could it be?

Shivers washed over me in waves. I tipped my glass and let more whiskey do its job. When I couldn't tolerate the cold any longer, I walked to the closet for a blanket. Staring back at me on the floor, propped against the wall, was a teddy bear. Considering I have no wife and children, the toy had no place in the apartment. *It belongs to the housekeeper.* Reasonable. *She couldn't get a babysitter and had to bring her child to work.* The logic felt thin, not to mention it was a lot like the bear that Toby's parents offered me. *You're talking crazy.* Still, the thought lingered.

The black marble eyes of the stuffed animal stared back at me when I extended my hand toward its nose. I half-expected the thing to jump at me like a bad special effect from a horror movie. I stopped short of the bear; positive it was ready to strike out at me. *It's just a toy.*

Gathering my courage, I lay my hand palm down on the bear's belly as if I were frisking the cuddly toy for a deadly weapon. Although I saw matted fur, the texture was soft and worn from the attention of a child over the years. I noted all the visceral details, and another sensation dug into my skin. It was a vibration— a low hum—spreading through my forearm and finally to my shoulder. As it turned from vibration to pain, I squeezed my eyes shut and tried to regain power over my body.

Opening my eyes, the glass windows of my apartment vanished. In its place were cinder blocks that lined my view in every direction. I was inside a basement and even smelled the dampness of the space. My heartbeat echoed in my chest.

Toby, I was sure it was Toby. He rested on a concrete floor. Embedded in the cement were steel chains. I followed the snake-like curving of the links with my vision until they ended up on the wrist of the small child. When I tilted my head toward the boy, he snapped his head my way and locked eyes to mine.

"Mommy?"

I wasn't sure if he really saw me, and I didn't care. I yanked my hand back from the teddy bear and saw the basement fall away as well.

Alone in my apartment, face to face with a child's teddy bear, Toby's voice echoed off the walls.

"Mommy."

I clutched my ears and pressed my palms into them to stop the sound of the child. To my horror, when my jaw fell open to scream, I realized the sound of Toby came from inside me like a stereo speaker.

Dale Evans had a house that sat on a sad little street. Everyone knew police officers didn't make enough and never would, but I felt sorry for the detective and his shabby little house. Dale swung his screen door open and flicked his porch light on in one motion. I stood there—arm outstretched, with a large zip-lock bag dangling from my fingers. The teddy bear stared from the bag.

"I don't even talk to my family this late," Dale said through squinted eyes.

I shook the bag as if the stuffed animal attempted a jailbreak. "Can I come in and talk?"

Dale stood as still as a statue.

"It's important."

After a long time, he gave me a nod to the house. "What's with the bear?"

"It belongs to Toby." Dale's expression turned from irritation to anger.

"What gives you the right to ask them for the bear?" Dale asked.

"I didn't." I shook my head to ward off his angry outburst. "The thing showed up at my apartment tonight."

"Bullshit. You think I'm stupid?"

"I'm not sure if you're stupid or not. But I found it at my house just the same."

He clenched his fists, but something stopped whatever he planned next, and he motioned me to his living room. I walked on wobbly feet to his couch.

"Can I sit?"

He ignored my question, so I sat anyway.

"You're shaking like a leaf. What the hell's going on?" Dale asked and sat on his chair in front of me.

"I saw a vision of Toby tonight."

"So what? Isn't that why we hired you for this case?"

I didn't know how to answer and stay in his home.

"I never had a vision..." I shook my head once more and let the words fall out slow, "before tonight."

Dale listened to my answer and studied my face until his eyes opened wide. "You son of a bitch. You've been faking this entire time. All of these cases? You gave these parents hope or dashed them when you didn't have a clue. You damn sure led us away from these missing children over the years," he said with venom clung to each word.

"This time I'm not pretending."

"Get your ass out of here before I throw you through the window." Dale stood over me and I thought I was dead.

"I'm not leaving," I said and put my hands up for defense. "I know I'm a liar—always *have* been. But I'm not this time and I can help you find Toby. Just give me a chance."

I could tell he wanted to punch me. Except he didn't. He eased himself back into his chair. "A parasite is all you are," he said, defeated.

"I know." I sat quietly for a long time, not wanting to push my luck. "All I'm asking is for you to watch me."

"What will that do?" Anger still colored his cheeks. "How's this going to work?"

Relief swept over me, and I presented the bag—with the bear inside—like a lawyer presenting evidence to a judge. I opened the zip-lock bag.

The smell of Toby wafted into the air. I wondered if Dale caught the child's scent. We sat across from each other like the beginning of a seance and I realized that was exactly what I wanted to happen.

"While I'm in the trance, I will try to describe anything I see. Maybe we can figure out where Toby is."

"Okay."

I took a deep breath, reached inside the bag, and pressed my palm onto the teddy bear's fur.

The vibration returned at once, and this time my location fell away much faster. One second I was in Dale's living room, and the next I was in the same basement I saw before. "I'm underground."

"Of a business?" Dale asked and the sound passed as if much further away. Like the other end of a tunnel instead of the same room. I shook his question away.

"It's the basement of a home. Cookie-cutter style. Cinder blocks all around me. It's a clean but unfinished basement."

"What else is down there?"

I scanned the small space and a part of me, where the fear lived, prayed Toby wasn't down there this time around. My hopes vanished when out of the corner of my eyes, I spotted him.

The chains remained, attached to his wrists. It was his eyes that drew my attention. Under them were bags so black that they appeared painful. He had been crying. Forever, it seemed.

"Toby is here. Shackled to a cement floor. He's naked except for underwear," I added.

"Is he alone?" That was a good question.

"No. Someone's with us." My skin went cold when a shadow passed by me.

"Who is it? Can you see the face?" Dale asked, and I heard his voice crack.

I was about to answer Dale when a feeling struck me. "Whoever's there can hear me," speaking no more than a whisper. There was no reason for me to suspect that the scene was anything more than a recording—played back. But I sat my finger to my mouth for Dale to be quiet.

The shadow of the figure loomed over the small child. I was almost positive it was a man.

"I want my mommy." Toby cried. And just like that, the shadow spoke.

"Your mommy can't help you," a gruff voice said. The shadow got bigger, which meant he walked closer to the boy. I felt so helpless and bit my tongue to keep from screaming.

I saw him extend a hand to Toby, and he was flesh and blood—a real person.

With his hand, he caressed his captive's hair while the frightened boy cried. "It's okay. You won't be here forever."

When the kidnapper rubbed the child's cheek, Toby clamped down on the man's web between his thumb and digit finger. When the man screamed, I could almost feel his pain as he jerked his hand back.

"Leave him alone, asshole," I screamed at the form, and he drew back into the shadow.

"What happened?" Dale whispered, and I ignored him. As I stared at the frightened, crying boy, a head leaned into my line of sight like an actor sliding into a camera frame. The face was strong, and I pictured him as a boy scout in his younger days.

"Who's there?" the voice from the other side asked.

My grip on the teddy bear tightened. The rest of my body also tightened with the sound of the captor. His tone was inquisitive, but I heard something menacing hidden underneath.

"I think he can hear me."

"That's impossible," Dale assured from outside my view.

"Oh…I can hear you both," the man's voice echoed in my ears.

"Shit," I blurted.

He moved closer to my face.

"I can see you, too. And your beautiful home."

A chill sunk into my spine.

"Let the boy go," I shouted in my most defiant tone. The man glanced over his shoulder at Toby.

"No thanks. I think I'll keep him. I'll come to visit you, though. You live in a corner home, right?"

Panic took me over, and I threw the bear across the room, disconnecting my view of the basement at once.

Dale's home was back all around me like a blanket. When I turned to his front window, a street sign sat on the corner in full view.

"I think we're in trouble."

"I didn't see or hear anything. You're still full of shit."

I shook my head.

"Explain this," I said and brought my hand up to his eyes. The web between my thumb and forefinger had tiny teeth marks. "Toby bit him and somehow it appeared on me, too." Dale pulled my hand closer—his jaw dropped wide open. He repeated my earlier word.

"Shit."

The bear was my link to Toby. That's what I told myself and Dale before I left his house. He didn't believe me. I mean, he was frightened shitless by the child's teeth imprinted into my hand— still, it was easier to think I found a clever way to make the wound myself. As for the kidnapper, the detective dismissed the idea altogether. When I told him he might know where he lives, he just laughed, then patted his holster with a gun resting inside.

My dreams were more vivid that night than they had ever been before. I spent years making up strange spiritual phenomena and when it started happening to me, I couldn't fully convince myself it was real. But the more I saw, the less I argued.

In the darkness of my apartment, I felt the teddy bear calling out to me silently from another room. It was like an itch I couldn't reach. Eventually, I'd retrieve the stuffed animal. I knew that too.

Ever since my interaction with the abductor, I sensed a connection between us. At first, it was a change in my temper, like I caught a cold from the guy. I swore I shared whatever mood or anxiety he experienced. Opening a portal between the two of us was illogical, but for him, it was inspiring, astounding. I could feel that.

My feet headed to the closet and the teddy bear I had stashed there when I got home. Was I in control of my body? The connection to the bear was strong.

I was a visitor in my flesh, and I stopped thinking as I opened the linen closet and snatched the child's toy.

The low hum that started all the links before was a screaming vibration. I placed my hands to my ears as if it would quiet everything. It didn't at all, and the portal opened in front of me, except it was dark. I stared at the blackness for what felt like minutes until my eyes adjusted.

I was in a new place—a bedroom. That much I made out. Mostly from the small amount of light that silhouetted the window next to the bed.

This was what I wanted to see. If I saw where the abductor lived, I could send the police there and save Toby before it was too late. My eye did better in the darkness by the second, and a form of him was coming to life on the bed.

The portal moved closer to the bed, and I rose and followed along like a kite tail along for the ride. *You're mine, asshole!* I was now floating above the bed with everything crystalizing.

The form in the bed was Dale—eyes shut—mouth drawn open in deep slumber. Why was I seeing Dale? My mind was foggy —slow to understand. I screamed through the portal when it all made sense.

"Dale? Wake up!" As I screamed, Dale's eyes shot open in time for another figure to jump onto the lower half of his body. The gestures were well-rehearsed.

A syringe sunk into Dale's neck, and I saw the lights go out. The abductor rotated himself atop Dale and positioned himself to the ceiling—toward me.

"Hey again," he said with a gruff voice.

There was so much mischief and violence in his grin that I had to close my eyes for a moment to regain control of my emotions.

"What did you inject him with?"

"Don't worry, the dose will wear off. With no damage to him. I came across the drug years ago. I'm told it mimics the toxin of an Australian stonefish. Have you heard of the fish by any chance?"

I kept quiet.

"Ugly little fish. Unaware beachgoers would step onto the fish on the shorelines. First comes the burning as the venom wraps itself into the skin and muscles. Soon begins the euphoria… compared to dropping acid. The body's muscles absorb all the poison until there's no trace left. But I plan on leaving a trace." As if by magic, his hand held a large knife. Dale didn't move, but his eyes saw it all.

"Get away from him," I shouted and instantly regretted the outburst. The sound of my scream made its way back to my ears.

"You spied on me. Now I will return the favor." The knife twirled between his fingers in a slight movement—rotated downward as he drove the blade into Dale's stomach.

The scene had a detached reality until blood poured from Dale's wound. More frightening than the aggression of steel plunged into flesh was how Dale didn't—couldn't react. His stone face hid all his suffering.

"That's not so bad. Right?" the intruder whispered to Dale. A smile returned to his face—much wider this time. "I rarely take this much pleasure in adults. I usually reserve my passion for the little ones. Thank you for this," he said and sunk the blade into Dale's neck.

Blood gurgled from his throat, and I saw his last breath mingled with red liquid. I couldn't stop my tears from falling as the murderer turned around to face me.

"I guess this is a game of leapfrog we're playing. You jumped onto my lily pad—I jumped onto Dale's lily pad. You're next." He ground his teeth. "I saw one of your old news spots on television tonight."

My blood went cold when I understood what he meant.

"I'm coming for you, Bryar Wilson," he said.

I flung the bear into the dark and severed our view of each other.

The moment I touched that bear, it sealed my fate. It was a matter of time before the killer came calling.

Detective Scott Sedge stared down at the teddy bear in the center of the living room. Blood matted down the fur of the stuffed animal and made a trail of crimson that circled the toy.

"Is it voodoo? I swear it looks like a ritual," Sedge asked a nearby officer in uniform.

"It beats me. We got a call that someone was screaming. But when I arrived on the scene there was no one here."

Sedge kept his focus on the marble eye of the bear.

"What's the name of the missing person?" Sedge asked.

"Bryar Wilson."

"The psychic?"

The officer nodded.

"Holy hell. I just talked to the guy," Sedge said.

"Heads up. There's another psychic assigned to this case."

"You mean to tell me we have a psychic investigating a missing psychic?"

"The order came from the captain himself," the officer said and handed Sedge the paperwork. "Here he comes now."

"I'm John," he said and reached with a hand until Sedge took it.

"Hey John. You ever heard of Bryar Wilson?"

"For sure," the young man almost shouted, "Bryar Wilson's the most famous psychic in the business."

"That's who we're trying to find."

"I modeled my career after his approach to psychic readings. He was the master."

"Now you have the chance to solve *his* disappearance," Sedge said and pointed to the teddy bear at their feet.

"I'm not sure if I can pick anything up in here," John said.

"Our captain thinks otherwise." Sedge nodded, then held back a laugh. "You do your best," Sedge said. "A detective, Dale Evans, was murdered in his home."

John swallowed hard.

"Bryar was last seen here before his disappearance."

John closed his eyes and extended his hand out into the air. "I got nothing. I'm sorry."

"Maybe you can touch something that belonged to the missing person. I saw that in a movie," Sedge said and laughed out loud.

"Sure. What do you have in mind?" John asked.

"How about the teddy bear?"

Sedge lifted the stuffed animal and extended it to the psychic. When the fur of the bear touched John's skin, his head fell back, and his eyes rolled into his head.

"I'm seeing a little boy with black hair. He's in a basement with shadows around him," John said and squeezed his eyes shut even tighter. "But there's someone else there."

"Just tell me what you see. Nothing there can hurt you," Sedge promised.

~ICE CREAM MAN~

My day begins the same every morning. There's nothing new to life. Nothing hopeful. I crawl out of bed and stumble over dirty clothes and empty pizza boxes. It's so hard to take care of myself and do the right things so someone will think I'm a great catch, but the same rut keeps finding me.

Reaching for the toothpaste tube, twisting for its precious last drop, I see Wendy's plant in the other room. I think it's a geranium, still couldn't say for sure. All I know is that it's turning brown. All her plants are turning brown. I brush my teeth and wonder if I can save the last memento of Wendy by watering it.

Rummaging through a pile of dirty clothes on the floor, I start my search for the garments without any stains, then start testing them with my nose. Selecting my wardrobe, I ignore the wrinkles. Who has the energy to get out an iron? Besides, I don't have anyone to impress, except a few brats that will pay, anyway.

Wendy used to make me breakfast in the morning. It wasn't much, two pieces of toast and two eggs. I like my eggs over easy. It's so great when you can dip the corners of the bread into the warm yolk and after all the yellow goodness is gone, I splash a generous helping of salt on the remaining egg whites and devour them.

Wendy didn't cook a lot and I guess that's why the small breakfasts mean so much to me. It was a tiny symbol of her love for me, or it was her appreciation for my grueling day ahead.

Anyway, I miss the gesture so much, and I miss *her*.

After I load up my ice cream truck with merchandise, I take the same route I've driven for the last seven years. I wanna try new streets. Just for the change of scenery, but I won't.

God, I want something new in my life! With all my wants, I know I will go the same way. These few side streets have made my living and I can't afford low sales with my finances the way they are. My goal is to prolong this point in my driving. Draw it out. But I do what I hate most. Ring the bell!

Ring…Ring…Ring

The stupid bell rings to bring out the vile little creatures who haunt my sleep. The ringing and ringing, the senseless ringing. The loud twang vibrates my brain as if it rings inside me, ripping at my very soul. As I pull the rope and watch the hammer hit the inside of the steel bell, my thoughts always, without fail, turn to my father.

My father was never there for me. One time he took me to his work when I was still young. He worked at a dog food plant. I can't recall which brand it was, but I will never forget the smell of the factory. Pungent is an understatement. He led me to where they slaughtered the animals.

A man in rubber overalls used a metal spear gun—driving it into the brain of cows. The beasts collapsed immediately. My father said it was the most humane way to end their life. That was so hard for me to grasp, and I guess it's hard to fathom even now. I thought you should prolong the death to give them a sense of closure, even if they didn't fully comprehend.

As my father guided me into the meat processing section of the plant, the aroma of rotting meat took me over. The vulgar smell of decaying flesh penetrated my nostrils. As I tried to inhale, my body functions worked against me. Vomit spewed from my mouth, catching me off guard.

My father stood there in horror. I'm not sure if it was his co-workers watching this that enraged him. As I gathered my senses,

I told him that the place smelled horrible. With an angry expression and equally angry tone, my father grabbed my arm and told me the unpleasant odor was the smell of money.

He never brought me to work after that, and I guess I don't blame him. And now, decades later, this wicked bell sounds like money.

As I turn left on Elm Street, I glimpse my first victims of the day following behind me. Some are on bikes and the rest run with flapping money in their grubby little hands.

The pleasure comes from letting them try to catch up to me for at least a block before stopping the ice cream truck. It's life's small pleasures that keep me going.

When the truck stops, sooner than my preference, I'm relieved to quiet the bell. Sometimes, what pops into my mind is the thought of slamming on the brakes. One of the children would smash into the back of the "Slow Children" sign fixed to the bumper. Resisting the urge is a struggle. I'm sure that the entitled children's parents might complain, and jobs are hard to come by.

Some of my ex-friends said Wendy moved into my apartment because she had nowhere to go. They thought she used me to get off the streets.

They don't understand Wendy as I do. She's a gentle angel. Anyway, I don't need friends anymore. I told them all to go to hell. Guess that's where they are.

Communication broke down between Wendy and me. When we first met, we were in harmony. I mean…we were perfect together. You couldn't pull us apart. But a few weeks ago, she started arguing with me.

I would say something to her, and she'd just stare at me. I wouldn't let that bring me down, though. So, I worked harder. Unfortunately, this didn't help matters much; she kept saying that I frightened her. I think when you really get into someone's mind, it must be scary. She just needs time to let everything I said sink in. She'll be back.

The little worms start in with all their high-pitched clamoring.

All of them more than likely have a freezer full of ice cream and popsicles—their rich parents buy it all to keep them quiet so they can drink screwdrivers and have affairs with their neighbors. The kids' allowances are more than I'll make in a week.

As usual, the first in line is the Parker boy, Todd, I think. He's the alpha of this group. He seems in charge. If he ever needs money, he bullies another of the smaller parasites to spring for him.

"What do you need?" I ask, trying to move things along. Kids will stand by my truck until the end of time if I let them. Buying a house is less of a chore than these kids picking a dairy treat.

The next one up is Josh. This kid annoys me to no end. Every day, he asks for something I don't have.

"You got any rainbow pops?"

"Dammit, Josh. You asked me this yesterday; I don't get rainbow pops. Just the pictures glued to the truck!" The little shit just shrugs like yesterday never happened.

I might be screaming that to him, I'm not sure, but he looks at me funny like Wendy has these past few weeks, and he walks away, buying nothing. He's a strange kid. When I finish handing out desserts, I notice the tip jar I fasten to the door is still empty. They're so ungrateful. I'll put a dollar in the jar, so they'll know what it's for.

Ring…Ring…Ring

This past week's been tough on me. Wendy loves me with all her heart, she just needs a reminder of what's important. She doesn't see me watching her sometimes. When we're back together, I'll tell her about my devotion to her, and she'll finally understand.

I'm the best thing for her; she needs to know this. I'm getting good at watching her. She doesn't do much during the day except go into her office. Lunch will come soon, and she goes out for lunch. Who knows, maybe I'll take some time from my busy schedule to talk to her.

Ring…Ring…Ring

As I pass out ice cream to these wretched kids, a policeman asks me if he could place a missing girl's photo on the side of my truck.

I don't want him to, but he will stare at me suspiciously if I don't agree. He keeps going on about children disappearing from the same route I deliver ice cream. I laugh at that. He watches me as if I have a second head, so I stop laughing.

I'm wondering if the police are out to get me. I see movies all the time where cops plant evidence or doctor something to frame a perfectly innocent person. That must be what they are doing, or why else would they visit me? But are they able to read my thoughts? Has it come to that yet?

Anyway, I'm thinking about Wendy a lot more lately. Our past together keeps returning to my mind. What did I do wrong? Then I remember that she's the one who messed things up—not me. Do I really want to give her a second chance?

Ring…Ring…Ring

Wendy finally comes out of her office for lunch. I park my truck so I can see her alone. A strange guy greets her with a kiss on the lips. I'm serious, it was right on her lips. She doesn't seem to care that we just broke up.

When I see the intruder, I decide to confront him for her. He's a bad dude. No doubt about it. I move from the truck and place myself in between them. There's so much fear in his eyes.

Without thinking, I let loose a punch into his face. Wendy pulls me off *him* and tells me to get away from *her*. As I head back to my truck, she apologizes for my behavior. She acts as if *I* did something wrong. When I turn back to say one more thing, Wendy says she will call the cops. I can't believe Wendy would join forces with the cops.

Ring…Ring…Ring

The drinks start early today. Vodka's my choice so no one can smell it on my breath. I bet I'm three sheets to the wind because I barely hear a parent complain about me driving over their child's bike the day before. I end the conversation by telling the parent to sue me if she wants to. To tell you the truth, one day feels no different from the last.

I sometimes find myself in places with no way of knowing how I got there. It's easy to not care anymore. To just let my urges take me over. I want that so badly. Is it the right thing to do?

Ring…Ring…Ring

When dusk finally arrives and I can go home, I notice a girl I recognize. Her older brother buys her ice cream from time to time. I see her in a running car—two men who own the car are close by and fighting about something. I turn in every direction to see if they notice me, and they don't. The neighborhood is quiet when I walk up to the window.

"Hi, little girl," I say to break the ice. She doesn't recognize me, and that's okay. "Would you like some ice cream?" I say in the sweetest voice I can pull off. The voice is working because she leans forward as I speak.

"You're the ice cream man," she says with a smile and moves to me. Although I see adults close by, I convince her to come out of the car and with me into my truck.

Ring…Ring…Ring

Later that night at the police station, I listen to the officer deliver some speech to me. I don't hear all that he has to say. I guess I care little for authority. He finally lets me go after, and he thanks me again for saving the girl from the stranger's car. The little girl's parents hug her with tears in their eyes. They thank me too.

I'm not sure what all the fuss is about. But I'm glad I can take the photo of the missing girl off my truck.

Ring…Ring…Ring

To my surprise, Wendy shows up at one of my ice cream stops. She looks pretty.

"I guess you're a celebrity now?" Wendy asks.

"I guess so. All the attention is weird."

She leans in closer, like she wants to kiss me. "You want to have dinner tonight?"

I nod, but her question shocks me. "What about the guy you're seeing?" I see the surprise change her expression.

"Trevor? It turns out he's an asshole. He acted like he was into me, then I never heard from him again."

"I'm sorry to hear he did that to you." I smile at her as bright as I can. "What time should I pick you up tonight?"

"Anytime is good with me. I'll see you later?"

I nod at her and watch her turn away with a smile.

"You want ice cream before you go? I know *Bomb Pops* are your favorite," I say, tempting her.

"Sure."

I reach into the deep freezer and see Trevor's eyes watching me. I think back to the day I brought him into the truck. It took forever to fit him in there. And way longer before he stopped thrashing. I push his frozen arm aside and hear it snap. Wendy hears it too.

"What was that?"

"A fresh start," I say and hand her a popsicle.

~MY SOUL TO TAKE~

I'm going to die today. If I could stop it—rewind history like a wristwatch and begin from the beginning—would I? Hell, we all would, I suppose. But what if death is a gift?

As I sat in a clinic, a pimple-faced assistant with onion breath approached me. He attached technology I didn't understand to my skull. This study, unlike others, paid a small fortune that I couldn't pass up.

"Is this gonna hurt, Doc?" He wasn't a doctor, but I said it anyway. The lab helper continued with his task of wiring me up like a toaster, and I let him do it for a price. I wanted a decent Christmas for my daughter Meagan, for once. I wasn't what you would call a stable parent. There is an unfortunate characteristic, deep in my DNA, I blame for my divorce. And it's the same flaw that took Meagan away from me except for monthly, *supervised* visits.

I like to drink. Nope, scratch that. I love getting drunk. I always have, ever since my first drink in college. That's right. I went to college for an entire semester, thank you very much. But when I placed that first beer to my lips at a freshman keg party... let's just say I guessed what I wanted to do for the rest of my life and threw it away at the same time.

The funny thing is, in my brief time as a college boy, I was undecided on a major. I never picked one. How could I? Something already chose me. 'Til death do us part, it whispered.

And the sentiment was right on the money because I'm dying here on a rocky slab, tasting alcohol along with the copper taste of blood. A new mixer for future drinkers. It comes with a cost, I'm afraid.

When the overachieving assistant left, a more suitable person to call *doctor* slid into his place. The more he talked, the more I thought about the bar I was heading to next and a toy store, if I could still walk by then. I might have saved myself if I took the man seriously. Probably not. But I would have had at least a shot of walking out the door.

"I guess you would like to know what you signed up for, am I right?" the doctor asked, scratching words onto a yellow notepad.

The guy didn't look like someone with a medical degree. If I had met him on the street, "sleazy lawyer" would fit the bill.

"I can't wait."

His smile widened. Another sign that said *run for the hills*. But I ignored that too.

"Have you ever had a dream where something or someone was trying to kill you?" A knowing smile transformed his face.

"All the time," I said.

He nodded, expecting the answer. "But in all of those dreams, did you ever die?"

I thought the question over and tried to recall such a time. "Never."

"There's an old wives' tale that says if you die in your dreams." He paused, turning on the theatrics. "You die in real life." He focused his eyes on me and waited for a reaction.

"Yeah. I think I heard that bullshit before," I boasted.

"That's what we're going to assess." When I opened my mouth to speak, he cut me off. "Oh. Don't worry. We are sure you won't die. What we want to do is test your brain when it *thinks* you died," he said, like they were already crafting his Nobel Prize in Medicine for his work in a shitty little clinic.

"Listen, Doc, I don't need to know how you make the peanut butter. Just spread the shit," I said, losing my temper. He threw me an expression that would stop a heart if it were able. I couldn't think of anything except having that first drink of the day, and the thing standing in my way was this bozo in a white jacket. He adjusted some dials, peeking back at me every so often.

"Most dreams are nothing but a fog fading into the air when you wake up. Not this one. You will remember every second as if you were wide awake," he bragged. He turned more knobs until the room started humming. It turns out, I was the one humming. One second the doctor was fiddling with his controls, and the next, I was gazing over a cliff, so high I couldn't see the bottom.

Things got real serious, real fast. I swiveled to see a desert landscape behind me that went on forever, then back to the mile-high drop that awaited me. You know the feeling you get in the pit of your stomach heading up the impossible slant of a rollercoaster? Multiply that by infinity. If I were standing there admiring the abyss in my mind, I would have pissed my pants all over the desert sand.

"I'm done now. Sir?"

A hand slammed into my back. And then I was flying. Not like a bird, but a rock. The distance down was so long the butterflies in the stomach had enough time to go away. I remember thinking, *I'm never going to land.* That's when I hit bedrock. A collision with all gravity's might.

With that velocity, things happen instantly. Like bones crush and organs smash. And any hope I had of survival dashed just like me against the rocks. I stared up at the stars with immense pain coursing through me. That's when I got a glimpse of a soul—my soul.

The soul radiated energy, and it was beautiful. The sarcastic asshole I had been my entire life melted away. I witnessed my soul slipping from my body like Saran Wrap off a sandwich.

The urge to reach out and grab it before it floated up like some wayward balloon at a carnival washed over me. And I remembered that I was too broken to move. I just watched my balloon, made of light, float up and away.

I was breathing, if you could call it that. My damaged lungs pushed out the air in short, raspy spurts until they stopped altogether. When I realized my lungs had failed, I panicked and tried manually circulating the air.

It was a no-go, and the soul became a dot within the starry night. My vision was the last to abandon me, and the stars above disappeared.

The next thing I remember was the doctor's smug face hovering above my gurney. I recoiled back into my pillow, relieved that my fate, crushed on the rocks, was nothing more than a wispy dream—more like a nightmare.

"See? Nothing to worry about," the doctor said.

"That was too real to be a dream."

The doctor's smile was everlasting. "We projected it into your mind. To you, it *was* real."

"Way too real," I whispered to myself. As I was drowning in the memory of the fall, he unbuckled my straps.

"Think of it this way," he began, still releasing me from the bed. "How many people get to experience death and still walk and talk afterward?"

"Once is enough." I didn't think it was possible, but his smile increased again.

"You can pick up your check in the front," he said.

Finally, a reason to smile back.

When I had my first drink of the day, the thought of my death lingered in my head like a fly bashing against a window, trying to get out and failing.

I wondered if it would ever dissolve or how having it as my companion might change me.

That kind of thinking was useless. *What's done is done.* The check was big, and I ate into it a bit by downing beer after beer. By the time I staggered off my stool, the world spun—just the way I liked it.

As I stepped from the bar, the failing light splashed shadows across my face. There was day left, and I drank faster than usual. I stared into the failing light, satisfied I'd accomplished something in the day. I was also determined to keep the party going, but at home. Picturing the bottle of bourbon resting on my refrigerator was the motivation to pump my legs harder to make it there before my buzz faded.

In my hurry to keep the celebration chugging along, I failed to notice an old guy blocking the path. Before I could stop my momentum, the guy was on his ass, and I was on mine. Laying there feeling stupid, my vision went dark. I swiveled my head in every direction and couldn't see a damn thing.

"What did you do to me?" I screamed at the older man somewhere in the darkness.

"You ran into *me*, son," he spoke, but I still couldn't see him or anything. When I couldn't stand the darkness any longer, light seeped in like a dimmer switch coming to life. What I was seeing played like a movie from some other time. I saw the old man standing in front of me at a bus stop. But this wasn't happening right now. I was experiencing some other reality.

"Hey, you?" I called to the old guy in the vision, but he couldn't hear me. Instead, he stepped off a curb as an arriving bus approached. The steel beast roared into the old man's path.

"Watch out," I screamed and swore he heard me as the bus, with immeasurable weight, plowed into the man, crushing him. As I saw his body mangled under the bumper, my vision flew away in a flash. When I tilted my head, the old man had me by the arm, bringing me to my feet.

"You're okay?" I asked, seeing him untouched by the bus.

"I'll survive, but you need to watch where you're walking," he said.

"The bus didn't hit you?" I saw the answer in front of me, but the urge to ask was too great.

"Nope. No bus hit me."

As I stood upright and took a step back, his glowing aura floated toward me. It resembled the same one from my dream in the clinic—the same golden balloon that floated into the atmosphere. This one wasn't drifting up. Instead, the thing wrapped itself around me like a cocoon. Its gold skin covered my flesh until it sunk into me, then it vanished from sight.

"Are you okay?" the old man asked me.

"I'm fine," I said, dusting myself off, already walking toward my apartment.

"Stay safe, young fella," a voice followed me as I left the scene behind.

Waking up in your puke isn't as glamorous as you might think. The chunks of vomit were mostly dry—that was good—but I smelled like bourbon still, from all the puke on my chest. The night before was a blur. I remembered making a beeline for the alcohol, and that was all—the rest faded in the fuzzy warmth of intoxication.

I pulled the shirt off me like it carried a disease and clicked on the television, focusing on the screen. I thought of showering off the vomit smell wafting from my chest. It entered my mind but didn't last long.

I sank into my chair and watched the flickering images of the local news. The volume was down, and I was happy to shift from one story to the next without the roar of sound. An image filled the screen that made me sit upright and scramble for the remote.

An accident scene filled the television screen with a bus in the center. I raised the volume way too loud but left it like that so I wouldn't miss a word. My vision from the day before came flooding back into my memory like a movie horror scene come to life. The field reporter showed the crumpled bumper on the bus—minus the body under it, of course. The bus driver said, "The old guy just walked in front of the bus. Seen nothing like it," he swore.

My chest seized when I saw the same bus stop from my vision. The old man died the exact way I pictured. Did I predict his death? I dismissed the entire experience as nothing more than a drunken hallucination.

But I couldn't do that anymore. That damn clinic gave me the power to see the future. Somehow my brush with death, simulated or not, awakened something in me. Something came through into the actual world.

Turning off the television and launching my frame from the chair, I headed to the shower. It didn't enter the front of my mind, but I refused to think about my newfound ability to see the future. Before my hair dried, I cleaned, dressed, and went through the door.

I needed food to dull the acid pain in my gut. I wandered into a fast-food joint without even thinking about the choice. My appetite guided my feet. The old man's death tumbled in my mind, and none of it made sense.

I shuffled in line as each customer ordered, then stepped aside like automatons. One way from my turn, and I heard my belly rumbling—ordering me to step on it. And that's when I got my first glimpse of the auras.

At first, it was nothing more than a halo over the customer's head, then I saw their body outlined in a bright illumination as well. I closed my eyes and tapped my feet to keep from shouting at the guy ahead to hurry his order. When I released my eyelids, the man a couple of feet in front of me screamed at the cashier.

"Open the register or you're dead," he promised.

I'm no hero, but the fogginess in my head from the auras, mixed with the young girl's frightened face, empowered me. I charged the assailant without a care.

From behind, I squeezed him tight and pushed him onto the restaurant's linoleum floor.

The move was more Saturday night wrestling than any actual skill, but the guy went down hard just the same. I gripped his wrist tight, and my vision went black like it had the day before.

The perpetrator was waving a gun at the officers, shooting his weapon from behind a car in the parking lot as if he were a gangster in a movie. I saw it all like a film projector flashing across a bedroom wall. After a few unsuccessful shots, the guy I was holding stood up in my prophecy in time to take a bullet in his forehead. The wound appeared like a third eye as he crumpled onto the pavement.

Sirens wailed. I let go of the robber just as my vision returned. *How long had I been holding him?* I saw no gun, but that's not proof he didn't have one. Instead of showing me, the guy shook his head and ran for the door.

When gunfire rang loud into the restaurant. I was sure he was dead. Again, I saw the future, and although I didn't want to admit it, as he escaped the scene I spotted his dark, golden cocoon floating toward me. He was the second person to donate their soul to me for safekeeping.

I wondered if death was their destiny, or I had something to say about their fates. These were bad guys, I decided. *I'm the Grim Reaper, dealing out justice.* I liked that idea. It made me feel noble. I wanted to tell everyone about my divine gift. But who could I tell? My bartender? My ex-wife and daughter? That would scare them.

I was alive with possibilities. I smiled to myself and thought of Meagan and how proud she would be when she knew her dad would finally do some good in the world.

When Julie, my ex-wife, called me *out of the blue*. It floored me. She'd seen me on the news and asked me to come visit Meagan during *unscheduled* time.

They live in the center of town, within walking distance. The sun shone high in the sky; the cicadas made their humming sound in the trees; a perfect summer day. The surroundings made me feel normal again and I was thankful, until I saw them. The auras were back and clinging to the townsfolk. With every person going about their day, their souls glowed brightly on their skin like shimmering diamonds.

I continued through the town, watching the souls undulate with the movement of their bodies like an invisible extension of the limbs. A toddler in the arms of its mother had a soul that shone twice as bright as the one holding him.

An older woman strolled past, and I saw her soul in a much darker shade. I can't say how I knew, but she was sick and close to death—I was sure of it. I read the health in each soul, and that scared me.

As a dog-walker with six dogs pulling her through the square scooted past, it astonished me to see the vibrant souls of the animals bounce and hop with their active little frames. I closed my eyes. I didn't want to see it anymore. All I wanted to do was make it to Meagan without thinking about my new cursed ability.

When I made it to the door, the relief in my heart was palpable. After a few knocks, my ex swung the door inward. She didn't say a word, like usual. I crept into the doorway as if entering the mouth of a whale. The place was no longer my home, and when I reached the living room, I felt like an intruder—an unwelcomed guest. Too many drunken nights turned the modest ranch-style home from mine into someone else's.

Shaking my head at where I'd ended up in life, I spied the couch I helped pick out.

"Can I sit?"

She thought it over and nodded. "You're late. You are always late," she said.

"Sorry. I've had a strange weekend. Good news though, I've come into some cash, and I will make sure you and Meagan get some."

Julie nodded but didn't seem to care.

"Where's Meagan?"

She bit her lip as if she were deciding. "Meagan," she shouted toward another part of the house.

The sound of little feet erupted on the wood floor, growing louder until I saw my six-year-old running toward me. Her face showed her delight, and she dove headfirst into my arms—a miniature Superman.

"Daddy," Meagan hollered. Her tiny body landed on my lap and against my chest. The sort of reunion I always hope for with my limited visits. As her soft skin rubbed against mine, my vision failed. Everything around me went black. *Oh shit!*

In my mind, I saw Meagan in the back seat of a car, bobbing her head along with the radio. The city street passed by in a blur, but she appeared happy and safe. *Maybe she'll be okay.* No sooner had the thought entered my mind, I heard the screeching of tires. Something was happening to the car, but my vision remained on Meagan.

The sound of twisting metal filled the inside of the automobile. Her little body shifted back and forth, jostled violently until the side of the car crushed her slight frame.

When my vision returned, I was crying. I wiped at my face and saw my baby girl alive and well in front of me. She wouldn't be okay for long.

"Are you okay, Daddy?" she asked. Even Julie flashed a rare expression of concern.

"I'm fine." I tried to pretend. I had to think about how to save her, and fast. If I saw the future, there must be a way to change it. But there wasn't enough information from the vision.

All I saw was her sitting in a back seat. There was nothing else. I couldn't point to a timeframe, and I had no way of keeping her out of a car for the rest of her life. I was out of options. Then, like a bolt of lightning, I thought of the clinic. The doctor could help.

"Meagan? Daddy forgot your gift." I tried to keep my voice even. The last thing I wanted to do was to scare her.

"You got a gift for me?" Her face lit up.

"I did, but dumb Daddy forgot it back at my apartment."

Julie gave me a sideways glance. She knew me too well.

"It will take me a minute to get it, though. Would you like that?"

Meagan nodded furiously.

"I'll go grab it and be right back," I said and stood up. When I did, I saw the golden balloon stretch from Meagan's body onto mine. In horror, I realized it was my touch. It wasn't prophesy. I took the souls and now I had snatched my baby's life force. Panic took hold of me as I remembered the fate of the old man at the bus stop. I hugged her again, hoping the soul would transfer back. It didn't.

"Are you really leaving?" Julie didn't understand, and I didn't have time to explain.

"I'll be back soon. I promise." And I kept promising until I was out the door.

When I slammed through the door of the clinic, the doctor dropped his boxes. They were full of files and pictures of patients, most of whom looked like me. His expression told me I'd caught him in the act. The furniture was no longer there. Anything that made the clinic a medical facility had disappeared.

"Where are you going in such a hurry, Doc?"

The doctor backed away into a wall.

"We're just done with our study. That's all," he said. I grabbed him by his white coat and slammed him onto the floor like he was a rag doll.

"What did you do to me?" I screamed, bouncing him off the floor once more. It loosened his tongue.

"There were side effects."

"What kind?" I clenched his clothes as a threat.

"If you die in your sleep—you lose your soul." He confirmed my worst fears. "You can't live without one so—"

"So, my body takes another. Like a vampire?"

The doctor nodded.

"This happened to others?"

"Yes," he said. "But we weren't sure until today. We verified other incidents."

I wanted to dig further, but I thought of Meagan.

"What can I do to stop the future deaths?"

The doctor threw me a blank stare. I flung him to the floor harder than before.

"Tell me!" I roared.

"I don't know. But I think you must kill yourself," he said with a whimper. He said out loud what I suspected. "Theoretically, if you die before your victim dies, then the soul that belongs to them will return to the rightful owner. In theory," the doctor said. I let go of his white coat, and he fell to the floor.

And this is where you found me. I stood on the edge of a cliff with a bottle of whiskey in my hand. There were a few swigs left, and that meant my time was near.

I clutched the note I'd written for Meagan, making sure it was still in my jean pocket—and it was. The spot appeared identical to the projection used on the patients in the clinic. I had no doubts.

As I thought one last time of the fate that awaited my daughter, I closed my eyes, stepped out over the edge, and found nothing but air. I plummeted to the rock surface below—the moment stretched an eternity just like before. The impact jolted my senses when I hit bottom. And as I stared up at the stars, taking my last breath, Meagan's soul floated up and away. *My gift is on its way, Meagan.*

~ LIGHTNING CRASHES ~

You might think spending an hour with the toilet seat at eye level might be the hint Cate needed—it wasn't. She threw up breakfas and dry heaved when her stomach was empty. Lunch went much the same.

A stomach bug was her first guess but the wrong one. By the time late afternoon came along, she had checked off all the boxes and suspected the unthinkable. Cate wasted one pregnancy test—watching it fall into the toilet—and made a trip to her local pharmacy for another box. *How hard can it be to pee on a stick?*

When the test came back positive, she still couldn't believe her eyes, rereading the instructions on the box to be sure. The hard truth sank in, and she walked around her farmhouse, trying on the idea of becoming a mom like a winter coat.

Cate had not even thought about how the child would end up. Those thoughts were for future Cate.

Pregnancy wasn't the end of the world. Cate liked the idea on some level, except it was *too* real and *too* soon. Newlyweds need time to get to know each other. Don't they? Her parents never had that "growing together" period, and they fought like cats and dogs her entire childhood until they finally gave up and divorced.

Dolion bustled through the doorway, scooping Cate up into his arms the way fresh husbands behaved, kissing her deep. When he let her go, she tried to hide her apprehension, but he picked up on it right away.

Unless you had months of planning, it all comes as a shock. It was a life-changing event that you suspect over a few days and confirm in a few minutes. Acceptance was a whole other challenge that Cate wanted before telling Dolion. She should have been ecstatic. The way her friends talked when she heard their news of pregnancy made it sound like it was always just part of their plan.

Cate didn't have a feeling that her life was coming together. That a new baby was the missing puzzle piece. Instead, an ominous veil fell over a moment that was supposed to be happy.

"Did I do something stupid?" Dolion asked.

Although her smile was genuine, her nervousness bubbled to the top. Their relationship was too new for him to detect it. She practiced the words in her head.

"That's a fantastic way to put it. Dolion, you did do something," she said.

Dolion circled her and found a nearby chair, flopping into it with all his weight.

There was an urgency to everything when you're a newlywed—no eggshells to walk on yet. They'd had minor fights over their short relationship but nothing to test them. This felt like a test to Cate.

Dolion stared at her like a man condemned to the electric chair.

"Cate. You're scaring me. What's wrong?"

When she realized her face mirrored the gloom she felt on the inside, she snapped out of her funk and gave him a smile.

"I'm pregnant," she said. She wanted to pretend it was exciting news, but it still sounded like the diagnosis of a disease.

Dolion studied his feet, then *her* feet, and erupted into the biggest laugh she ever heard from him. Dolion picked her up into his arms and swung her around the living room.

"That's great news," he said.

"I thought so, too," Cate said, uneasy. Dolion stopped swinging her and set her back onto the hardwood floor.

"Swinging you like that won't hurt the baby, right?"

Cate glanced at him to see if he was joking, but he wasn't. She couldn't stop the laughter.

"We're safe for now," Cate said through giggles.

Cate sat up in her bed as a tingle started in her belly. It was no more than a twinge in her skin. She wasn't far enough along to sense anything of a human life other than the hormonal symptoms of pregnancy. But her mind filled in the blanks for her, and she imagined movement when there was none.

Dolion lay next to her, dead to the world, as she slid the quilt off her legs. She let her eyes fall onto her husband and his bare shoulders that peeked out over the quilt. She wasn't sure how she expected Dolion to react to her having a baby, but he had taken to the idea far easier than she imagined. His exuberance was so startling that it felt as if he planned the entire thing, and she was nothing more than an unwilling participant.

Cate pushed the negativity aside and dropped her feet off the bed to the floor below. A chill ran up her spine as her toes touched the coldness of the wood floor. More than the temperature alone, Cate felt an uneasiness drown her senses.

She scanned the moonlit room and found herself alone with her husband, but it was as if eyes were watching her. The feeling was foreign, but it was there, pressing down on her.

She positioned her foot flat on the ground, with each step resembling a mountain climber. Dolion's snoring rose and fell, and the wooden floorboard kept on creaking.

Cate moved forward, but toward what? Her body knew, but it wasn't letting her in on the surprise.

There was an elusive quality to the voyeur, like a suitor across a dance floor deciding if he wanted to dance or just watch the night away from afar.

Cate half-realized she wasn't wearing a single thread. She passed the windows with moonlight streaming inside, bathing her naked body with its glow. The tingle in her stomach returned as if the light set off a reaction. It caused her to think of her belly as someone else's instead of the one she'd known her entire life.

The watcher's intensity continued stronger than before, and she thought of a farmer buying a horse and scrutinizing over every body part. The sensation made her feel cheap, as if she were no more than a specimen under a slide.

Although her mind lingered in a fog, her path led her to a round area rug leading to the front door. To her shock, both she and Dolion had left the door wide open all night. From the gaping doorway was the view of a tree. Dolion's great grandfather had planted the tree that stood high above their property.

The surrounding air became charged and filled everything with static electricity. Even Cate's tongue had the taste of copper. Electrical particles danced through the atmosphere like dust through a ray of sunshine.

As if a movie played, Cate trained her vision onto the mighty tree a second before a bolt of lightning flashed across the sky, illuminating the black skies. The rod of electricity struck the tree, and the trunk of the tree exploded in a cascade of sparks. The fire spread from the trunk to the branches in an instant.

The watcher wasn't laughing at the scene, but she got the idea it took enjoyment in it—a family legacy going up in flames. The fire moved from the tree to the long grass, increasing at an uncomfortable pace toward her.

The fire was a beast, eating, devouring everything in its path until it reached the porch. The flame consumed the wooden swing, the walkway leading to the screen door, and finally the door itself. The urge to scream for Dolion was immense, but she stood there on the area rug watching as the flames entered the house and consumed her. She opened her mouth to scream, and it was Dolion's voice she heard.

"Cate?"

The flames crashed the roof in on her—that was her first thought when Dolion shook her. Cate was naked and stood on the rug a few feet from an open door. But there were no flames, and the tree Dolion's great-grandfather had planted stood unharmed.

"Dolion?"

He pulled a blanket off the couch and covered her while moving them away from the door. "You're freezing. What are you doing out here?"

She didn't have an answer. Telling him about her nightmare was her next move, except it didn't feel like a nightmare, and superstition told her if she spoke about her vision, it might come true.

"When I didn't find you next to me, I got scared," Dolion said.

"Next to you?" she repeated.

Dolion walked his wife back to the bedroom with a blanket draped over her shoulders.

"We got a phone call." Dolion sat her on the bed, slid the blanket from her, and guided her under the bed's quilt. Cate couldn't make out every detail of his face, and that spared her some pain.

"It was about your mom and…" He paused. "There was an accident."

"My mom?" Cate asked.

"On her way here to see us…a truck going the wrong way on the highway—" When Dolion pulled her into his arms, her body went limp.

"Mom?"

Her belly grew and started to make her normal clothes tighter. She wanted to be happy about buying maternity clothes, but the idea felt repulsive. She was sure maternity clothes never flattered a woman's form any more than a potato sack might accentuate the produce inside.

Her mother was on her way when she died. What she lost was more than someone sitting beside her and guiding her through a pregnancy. She had lost a good protector.

After her mother's death the feeling of *watching eyes* never let up. The thought of someone spying on her destroyed her intimacy with Dolion. She didn't want to do anything personal—private—anything with meaning for the watcher to see.

The clacking of footsteps came first, then Dolion leaned through the bedroom doorway, torso hovering in the opening like a ghost floating in midair.

"You have a guest," Dolion announced as he leaned into their bedroom.

Cate stared at him as if he had never spoken aloud. Her position in the bed hadn't changed since he checked in on her hours earlier and she didn't care.

"Reverend Jones," he said.

The reverend walked past Dolion, smiling ear to ear.

"She hasn't taken a meal away from the bed since her mother died," Dolion tried to whisper but she heard. "I'll leave you two alone," Dolion said to Cate and vanished into another room.

Reverend Jones edged into the bedroom, noticed a chair against the wall, and plucked it as he went toward the bed. He situated the old kitchen chair close to Cate.

"I wanted to stop by and congratulate you on your arriving bundle."

She kept her sight on him, but pushed toward the headboard.

"Dolion tells me you haven't really eaten since your mother's passing. I know it seems bleak now, but God has a plan for everything—"

"It wasn't God that killed my mother." Her words echoed off the small bedroom walls.

Her response threw him back into his chair before it came out from under him—finding the floor before he could stop his fall. He scrambled off his knees, placing his bottom back on the chair, embarrassment coloring his cheeks.

"Who killed your mother?"

"You know damn well who was behind it," Cate said with venom thick in her throat.

"Cate. I don't." He reached toward her and rested a comforting hand on her arm. When she peered down at his fingers they were without skin. Rotting meat clung to his knuckles and joints. Along with the horror of seeing the bone through his flesh, heat scorched her arm. Raised blisters formed where his hand rested. She screamed from the searing heat.

"Get your hands off me," she said and covered her arm from his touch.

Reverend Jones obeyed, checking his hands as if his grasp contained melted iron instead of flesh and blood.

"Don't you ever touch me," Cate said.

"I won't," he said, shock transforming his face. "Maybe I overstepped my bounds. I only wanted to comfort you."

"Dolion! Dolion?" Her voice cut above everything until her husband's thundering footsteps captured all the sound. He stepped to her side and saw her writhing in pain.

"What's wrong?"

The reverend put his hands in the air.

"Get this son of a bitch out of here. Make him leave, Dolion," Cate said, still writhing on the bed. Dolion never said a word to the reverend, ushering him from his chair to the doorway—away from Cate.

When she was alone, Cate studied her arm and found angry red blisters forming the outline of a hand.

Cate sat by the window in her bedroom. She'd been staring out for a long time and didn't hear Dolion's approach.

"I brought something for you to eat," he said and slid a silver tray with a cover like hotels used for room service. "I was worried."

Cate was worried as well. She couldn't remember the last meal that wasn't nauseating to look at or one she finished that didn't end up in the toilet.

She watched her stomach grow but her body was going the other way. The extra weight that she started with when she found out she was pregnant shrank. Bones protruded from her knees and elbows the worst. But other areas caused a frightened look in her husband's expression. It was her chest and collarbone that made him turn his head away most times.

Babies live off their host. The idea was nothing new to Cate but the idea of it as a parasite took on more urgency as she saw her figure vanish by the day.

Dolion lifted the silver dome off the tray. Light hit the food.

"Oh shit," he said and slumped. The plate contained a healthy helping of potatoes, a buttered roll, and a steak so rare that blood ran over all the side dishes. Bright red blood pooled on the tiny plate. "I am so sorry. I thought I cooked the steak perfectly. Don't touch it. I will whip up something else," he promised as he was already through the doorway.

"I'm fine. Don't bother," she said to the empty room. Her words sounded weak to her ears.

She sat staring at the food pooling in a pond of blood. She waited for the sight of the plate to work on her gag reflux the way every other meal had done. But it didn't.

Cate moved closer to the abandoned tray and picked up the meat with her fingers. A trickle of red cascaded down her wrist and she licked it before it travelled down her elbow. Her eyes went wide when salt and copper spread over her tongue.

She sunk her teeth into the steak and tore at the meat until a generous chunk sat in her mouth. As she chewed, the juices ran down her throat like squeezing a sponge dry. The flesh mixed with the blood heightened her senses and she recognized the return of her appetite after so long.

She lost herself in the urge of eating as she tore at the meat and greedily swallowed. In the swoon of the deluge, she didn't hear Dolion return. He stood still and watched blood dripping down her chin and soaking her shirt.

"I want my meat like this," she said with some discomfort flashing across her face. "It must be the minerals or vitamins of the uncooked meat I'm craving."

He sat down on a chair across the room and stared at her for a long time, wanting to say things but not ready to disturb her peaceful mood, a rarity.

Cate did a horrible job at wiping her cheeks and looked to Dolion. "Something is coming," she said.

"Our baby," Dolion whispered.

She shook his words away, staring out at his grandfather's tree. Its branches reached toward the heavens.

"There is something in this house with us. Can you feel it the way I can?" she asked. She was sure he could. "A cloud has moved over us."

"It's just the hormones. It's natural," Dolion said.

She turned her head to the side and gave him a flash of disgust before returning to her view of the tree.

"Am I going crazy?"

He bounded to his feet and wrapped his arms around her, and she let him.

"Just a bump in the road," he said and placed his hand on her stomach, feeling the baby kick.

Cate was close to tears when the medical technician rolled a tower of equipment to where she lay. Resting above was a monitor, and extending from its side was a wire with a probe at the end. Dolion clenched her hand tight as the technician drizzled clear gel onto the head of the probe and pressed it onto Cate's bare belly.

Cate squished her face as the operator clicked and snapped buttons while they all watched.

"What were your issues? We can't squeeze patients in unless there's a critical concern."

They both fell silent. Cate thought of what her answer might e but pushed the ugly thoughts aside.

"Something is wrong with my baby," Cate said.

"Do you feel any pain?" the technician asked.

Cate turned away and shook.

"I need to know if my baby is deformed."

The technician froze in place, a glance going to Dolion and back to Cate.

"Excuse me?" the technician asked.

"I dreamt it was an insect. A larva wriggling inside me," Cate said. "Have you seen that in a pregnancy?"

"Not once," the technician said.

The examination continued with a grainy picture bursting onto the monitor. "There are cases of children forming wrong but…" The live images of the baby filled the screen.

"Here's the head—arms—legs, and everything is perfect."

Cate watched the images on the screen and cried.

Pain shot through Cate's body and woke her from a rare peaceful sleep. The jolt sent her to a sitting position on her bed. She was naked, with the covers off the mattress, and Dolion's usual spot empty.

She breathed heavy, feeling her chest move in and out and thought of Dolion. During the beginning of her pregnancy, he was attentive to her every need. But it wasn't until she saw a shift in his behavior that she wished for the early days.

As her anxiety increased, Dolion spent more time away from her, sometimes not sleeping with her at all. Cate was sure she pushed him away, but there was a coldness she detected from him when he interacted with her. She thought she was being stupid, but the idea persisted.

Her belly exploded with agony as it never did before. She watched her swollen stomach dip and stretch from the inside. The violence that stirred inside caused her to scream. The baby wasn't just moving inside her, it felt more like a crawling sensation like it was on its knees in the small space.

When the pain became too great, Cate leaned back on her pillow but kept her eyes down at her undulating belly that jolted upward. It was the way a cat arched its back, but she knew an unborn infant couldn't do such a thing.

A scratching started inside her, and the lump moved toward her crotch.

"What the hell?" she asked and gripped the mattress tight.

Another jolt told her that the baby was trying to crawl its way out. When she felt something pass through her canal, it was all too clear. "Don't, it's not time," she begged.

The pressure and hurt were too much as the infant slid its way from inside her into the night air and plopped on the bed next to her feet.

With the pain subsiding she leaned her head forward in time to see the child crawling between her legs. The umbilical cord dragged behind the small thing.

Cate couldn't see the child's face in the darkness. Only a small form on all fours appeared as it landed onto her belly and slid up her body.

When she turned her head she saw Dolion in the mirror. He sat in a chair next to the bed. There was so much joy on his face as he watched the scene unfold.

When Cate woke, she wasn't in her bed as she thought but in a rocking chair next to the window.

She rocked back and forth, hoping the constant movement would make her feel sane. The thought of her baby tearing its way out of her fell into the background—if she kept rocking.

Dolion lay asleep in a chair next to the bed.

"It never leaves me," Cate said. "It watches me a little each day, but *it* is always by my side now."

"What is?" Dolion asked in the room, silent except the chair's swing.

"I didn't know it, but it was preparing me. All of it. It killed my mother. It separated me from my church; even from you," she said.

"Who are you talking about?" Dolion asked.

"The devil," she admitted.

Dolion shook his head in disgust.

"If you need me, I'll be outside." Dolion was gone before she could answer.

The sound of the screen door slamming hard against the frame let her know he was gone and that he didn't believe her.

"Help me, Dolion." Although her husband was close, she knew it was far too late. Too late for everything.

The wicker bassinet sat in a corner. That was all she saw for a long time until something stirred inside the baby bed. The thought of the word "it" flooded in as her eyes adjusted. Something sprouted from the head. She saw its glowing red eyes and knew she was back in a dream.

"What are you?" Cate asked.

The creature ignored her as it reached its hand outside of the crib. Her heart fluttered, and she jerked her body away from the thing in the dark.

She strained against every muscle to avoid launching herself from the bed. "Stay away from me," she screamed.

"Don't you know me?" the creature asked, in a voice like razors rubbing onto vocal cords. It leaned over the edge of the bassinet to stare into Cate's eyes.

"I don't know you," Cate screamed. The creature tilted back into the shadow of the bassinet and beamed back to her from the blackness.

"You will."

Cate lurched from her bed, sweat pouring from her. Her eyes darted from her bulging belly to the bassinet that lay empty.

Static electricity charged the air, and her tongue had the copper taste again. Walking onto the area rug, Cate watched the mighty tree as a bolt of lightning flashed across the sky.

The rod of electricity struck the tree, and the trunk exploded in a cascade of sparks just as it did in her dream. When the pain in her stomach rose, she knew the time had come at last.

"Dolion," she called out into the night. She didn't have to check to know liquid flowed to the carpet below. *My water broke.* That was her thought, but another idea came to the front.

"I get to see you with my own eyes," she whispered.

When she looked outside she saw the wind whip across the landscape. What had been building up the last nine months was close. She felt it the same way she felt the wind upon her cheeks.

The strange occurrences that haunted her came in and out in waves. When she could stand it no longer, the horrors ebbed away. But she knew it would return.

The branches in the nearby trees swung; a mirror of the rising wind and the clouds above took on a menacing swirl that was terrifying.

A flash of lightning cut through the sky and sliced into the tree Dolion's grandfather planted. The sky went as bright as daylight before returning to normal. The bolt tore the tree in half down the center like the hand of God tearing a stalk of celery apart. The lightning that caused the fire spread from its trunk to the branches, but her mind told her the fire was always there, waiting to escape.

The wind gushed harder, and Cate screamed for her husband once more, and this time she saw him running for the house.

His sturdy legs went wobbly as he ran. The thunder roared and everything shook. She saw him tossed to the ground.

Thrown to one knee, Dolion found his feet and he got a steady sprint toward the front porch and Cate.

When he pulled the door open, she saw his horror as red liquid circled her on the floor. The area rug she lay upon was the shade of her blood.

Cate heard someone enter the house, but her vision betrayed her. One second she watched Dolion standing in the doorway and the next she stared at the ceiling above. standing

The only thing that was real was a pain that began in her stomach and shot out through her limbs.

"Dolion?" Her voice was soft, like speaking through a blanket.

"I'm here," Dolion said and squeezed her hand. "I called the doctor." He placed a pillow under her head, and she saw him for the first time.

"Am I okay?"

She watched him look down at the lower half of her body and back to her with an expression he couldn't hide if he tried. "Is it that bad?"

He didn't answer. Even as her vision fogged she knew he was frantically doing something around her.

"I think the baby's coming," she said with no more urgency than announcing the start of a television show.

His movements stopped.

"What's happening?" Cate asked.

She glimpsed Dolion slide a blanket off the couch, then felt it as he pushed it under her legs.

"We can do this," he announced with a renewed rush of optimism shining in his voice. "It's here. It's visible."

"It hurts so bad."

"Just keep pushing."

With a few more screams from Cate, she saw the child resting in Dolion's hands.

"It's fine. He's perfect," Dolion said with a smile.

"Good," she said. "Now kill it."

Dolion stared at his wife in disbelief.

"You heard me. Kill that evil thing."

Dolion brought the child closer to his chest. His face turned to rage.

"Do it," she said with more force than before.

Dolion stood up with the infant and walked toward a nearby bedroom. Cate listened to the sound of running water and after a long while, the footsteps led back her way.

"Is it done? Did you drown it?" she asked, sweat dripping off her face.

"You've lost a lot of blood," he said, close to her but just out of view.

Cate strained her body upward as much as she could and let her head sway toward the floor. She spotted the blood pooling around her. Twice her size.

"Oh God. Is the doctor coming?"

Dolion kept his silence.

"No," he finally answered.

"What?"

"I never called the doctor. He won't be arriving."

His words made no sense until he stepped close and leaned over. Holding the baby in his arms—its little frame pointing her direction—she saw its face. And when the child opened its eyes they were red like in her nightmares.

"Why is it still alive?" Cate asked and saw the reason. As she shifted her view of the infant's eyes, she saw Dolion with eyes as red.

"I had nine months to bring you around," he said. "But it didn't happen."

"What are you saying?"

He stood close but remained quiet.

"Dolion. I'm cold," she said with her strength failing her.

"It won't be much longer," he whispered.

As Cate's vision dimmed, she saw her child stare back at her. She couldn't be positive in her last moments, but she thought she saw the infant smile. A slight upward turn from the side of its mouth and that was all.

ABOUT THE AUTHOR

Jerry Roth is an author best known for his horror novel *Bottom Feeders*, and his thriller *On the Tip of Her Tongue*. Jerry currently lives in a small town in Ohio with his wife and two children. He lives in a 1908 catholic church—now converted to a home. You can learn more about the author at:

www.Jerryrothauthor.com

Facebook: @jerryrothauthor

Instagram: @_jerryroth_

Twitter: @_jerryroth_

ABOUT THE ILLUSTRATOR

Kealan Patrick Burke is the Bram Stoker Award-winning author of *The Turtle Boy*, *Kin*, and *Sour Candy*. He lives in Ohio with his crazy dog in a house that likes to pretend it's haunted. Visit him on the web at www.kealanpatrickburke.com or on Twitter @kealanburke

ACKNOWLEDGEMENTS

This novel is for all the fans of my horror work that patiently waited for me to return to the darkness after I indulged in other escapes.

A large part of this collection was born in the 80's and 90's and it's exciting to bring the sensibilities and stories of long-ago decades to a modern audience. Some of these tales, *Ice Cream Man* being one of them, came from my first college class. That student way back when would never believe it would end up in a published book. I'm forever humbled.

I want to thank Heather and Steve Vassallo for believing in my writing and helping me bring this collection out into the light. Their passion for stories is an inspiration to me. There are great things coming from Brigids Gate Press. Of that I have no doubts.

And to my family, for which none of this could ever happen without your love and patience, I want to tell my children Jesse and Lea that anything is possible if you keep trying.

MORE FROM BRIGIDS GATE PRESS

Visit our website at: www.brigidsgatepress.com

Whether in an old weathered mine shaft, somewhere off the beaten path, out in the woods, or right here in the middle of this ghost town, danger awaits. We're going to take you way back, drop you right smack dab in the middle of the Old West at its finest. But we're not just going to give you shootouts and bullet wounds and blood splatter. Yes, those things are prominently featured, but there's so much more to this anthology of western horror.

Maybe it's a well-known creature popping in for a visit, or some new creepy crawly monster sucking out your soul, we're going to turn the Old West inside-out and explore its guts to the fullest. There are new adventures to be had, monsters both familiar and unfamiliar to be thwarted… And we're not always going to be the victors. Life in the Old West is hard, trying at its best, and it can wear you down quick.

So, prepare yourself to be transported back in time. Get yourself up on that rickety stagecoach, draw your guns, and let's get going. There's vast territory to cover here, and your journey begins now.

Medusa.

Cursed by the gods.

Slain by Perseus. A monster.

So the poets sang.

The poets got it wrong.

Daughter of Sarpedon: A Tempered Tales Collection is an anthology of short stories, poems, and drabbles, ranging from retellings to completely new stories, from ancient to modern day.

Arthur, whose life was devastated by the brutal murder of his wife, must come to terms with his diagnosis of dementia. He moves into a new home at a retirement community, and shortly after, has his life turned upside down again when his wife's ghost visits him and sends him on a quest to find her killer so her spirit can move on. With his family and his doctor concerned that his dementia is advancing, will he be able to solve the murder before his independence is permanently restricted? A Man in Winter examines the horrors of isolation, dementia, loss, and the ghosts that come back to haunt us.

Decades after his grandfather was buried alive in a Californian gold mine, Dr. Nick Jones teams up with an adventure travel influencer to venture underground and film a documentary, telling the story of what really happened.

What should be a dream come true soon becomes a nightmare as someone or something stirs…BELOW.